About the author

James Warden was a teacher for forty years, and retired in 2006. He now enjoys his retirement as much as he enjoyed his time in the education service, and is catching up on those things which he left undone and ought to have done – in particular, his writing. He writes every morning between nine o'clock and noon, for thirty-six weeks of the year.

He is fortunate enough to be able to act in several Norwich theatres – the Maddermarket, the Sewell Barn and, with the Great Hall Players, at the Assembly House – and this experience informs his writing. His stage adaptation of Laurie Lee's *As I Walked Out One Midsummer Morning* was performed at the Sewell Barn Theatre in November 2009.

James is married – for the second time – and lives in Norfolk. He and his wife travel as much as possible. They have visited Italy (where they were married in 2002) several times, Canada, Bermuda, Egypt, India, the Czech Republic, New England, Poland and Slovenia. They have also taken several holidays in various Mediterranean resorts – the basis for his first novel, *Three Women of a Certain Age*, which was published in July 2010.

During his years in education, he wrote about twenty play scripts for children. These included the one that formed the basis for his children's story, *The Great*

JAMES WARDEN

Gobbler and his Home Baking Factory at the North Pole, which he wrote in 1982 and published in December 2010.

He has three sons by his first marriage and they inspired two of his novels – *The Vampire's Homecoming*, which was published in 2011, and *The One-eyed Dwarf*, published in 2012. With them and his first wife, he also travelled to the southern states of North America, France, Germany (West and East), Estonia and what was Czechoslovakia.

The Age of Wisdom

by
James Warden

Grosvenor House
Publishing Limited

This book is published by
Grosvenor House Publishing Ltd
28-30 High Street, Guildford, Surrey, GU1 3EL.
www.grosvenorhousepublishing.co.uk

A CIP record for this book
is available from the British Library

ISBN 978-1-78148-974-1

To
Jane, who spoke out
and
Graham, who remained silent

Chapters

Characters

Andrew Mansell	(47) headteacher of Foxhall Primary School
Mary Mansell	(46) primary school teacher
Jonathan Mansell	(22) has completed university and is about to take a 'gap' year
Robert Mansell	(20) about to start his 3rd year of a 4 year course at Newcastle
Amy Mansell	(18) has just started at Essex university.
Madge	(called Lady by Andrew), their cocker spaniel
Derek	the father of Mary's older brother's wife
Julian Price	(44), headteacher of Park Avenue Primary School
Elaine Price	(42), primary school teacher
Rosemary Price	(14)
Matthew Price	(9)

Staff at Andrew's school:
Jack Tate
Megan   Deputy Head

Clodagh······················supply teacher
Elizabeth (called Lizzie)
Antonia

Staff at Julian's school:
Edith Spence··················Chairlady of the Governors at
·····························Park Avenue Primary
Emily Saunders················Deputy Head
Jodie Smith················the 'other woman' (referred to
·····························as Little Miss Lovematch by
·····························Jack Tate)

Sue··························Mary's headteacher

Relations of the Mansells:
Elspeth···················Mary's sister
Brian·························her husband

Friends of the Mansells:
Dennis Dawson
Mona Dawson
Shaun Nesbitt
Gilbert Rouse

The year is 2010 - 11

Book One

CHAPTER 1

Unhappy enough

"Have you seen this?" asked Mary Mansell, passing the paper across the table to her husband as they sat after dinner.

"Yes," he replied, without looking up.

"You haven't looked."

"It's the report on Julian's death, isn't it?"

"Aren't you interested?"

"Yes."

"Then why don't you read it? ... Oh, don't bother. I'll clear away the dishes – someone has to. You're very close, these days."

Andrew Mansell ignored all three barbed remarks, but picked up the newspaper his wife had left, while she bustled about, knocking against it as she cleared the table. Andrew glanced quickly down the centre of the report, taking it all in at a glance – a habit he had developed in order to survive the barrage of paperwork that had poured in from the Department of Education for over a quarter of a century. He then turned his attention to the whole article, which he found terrifying in its conciseness.

'*Tributes have flooded in for a former teacher found dead at the weekend. Julian Price, 44, had been head of*

Park Avenue Primary School for five years. His body was found on the railway line at Westerfield Station on Sunday night, and he is thought to have taken his own life. Former colleagues at Park Avenue Primary School learned the sad news on Monday.

Edith Spence, Chair of the Governors, said: "Julian has worked here for five years. It's a huge shock. He was loved by the staff, children and parents alike, and has had a tremendous impact on our school. It has been a shock because we never thought he was the kind of person to do that sort of thing.

His estranged widow, Elaine, of Sunningdale Avenue, said: "Julian was a much-loved husband and father. We were together through many of life's trials and tribulations. My heart is broken, knowing that he was unhappy enough to do this." Mr and Mrs Price had two children, Rosemary, aged 14, and Matthew, aged 9.

After 23 years together, the couple split up. Mrs Price said her husband had suffered from depression. He is believed to have recently ended a relationship with a new partner.

An inquest into his death has been opened and adjourned.'

Andrew Mansell had known Julian Price as a colleague, and he knew Elaine more closely because they worked in the same pyramid of schools. He was surprised that the news had not shocked him when Elaine's headteacher had phoned it through, quickly, on that Monday morning – but it hadn't. It wasn't that he had expected Julian to do anything so disastrous and irreversible, but that he had listened, second-hand, to accounts of the marriage break-up as they filtered through from the staffroom at the time.

He couldn't begin to imagine what Elaine might be going through, and refused to pretend that he even began to understand. He was already annoyed by the speculation which was lurching from school to school, and angry with his wife who was obviously eager to pump him for information. Andrew got up from the table, and slid quietly through to his study, which was on the ground floor at the back of the house. He kept a coat in there for when he walked the dog. Slipping it on and giving the spaniel a nod, he stepped out through the french windows and walked quickly down to the back garden gate. He hoped he had disappeared, along the alleyway that lined the side of the house, before any of his family noticed.

Across the road was Christchurch Park and a half-an-hour or so of freedom; it was a favourite place of his, and the dog enjoyed their frequent walks. As he approached the park, passing by his local – The Woolpack – Andrew changed his mind and strode off along Westerfield Road towards the village and its station. It wasn't any fascination with the macabre that drove him, but a desire to know – to look into the 'heart of things'.

It was a beautiful evening captured somewhere between late summer and early autumn, and he enjoyed the sense of being caught within its glow. The horse chestnut trees on the park had just turned, and the other trees would follow in their proper order. A clutter of young starlings was pulling at some berries. Their plumage was in that half-way stage between chicks and adult bird – their bodies grown up, their heads still young. They were tucking into the berries and enjoying each other's company – young birds together.

He crossed the old bypass of Ipswich and made his way down the Westerfield Road. He had cycled along here as a boy, and he still remembered the sounds and sights of the countryside when he passed between the hedges – woodpigeons gleaning, mushrooms growing through the stubble, the smell of new-mown hay and tractors turning over the potato harvest. It was busier now with cars hurrying between the town and the village, and Andrew's nose was invaded by the sharp tang of petrol fumes.

You don't look back. The future looms forever forward, and you have to get on with it. How, he wondered, was Elaine Price 'getting on with it'? It was a phrase handed down from his parents' generation – the war-time generation – who *had* to get on with it. Life wasn't the same now, however: there were options which had not existed before – at least not for his class of people, not 'on the whole', not 'in the normal run of things'.

He recalled, for the second time that evening, how the tittle-tattle had spread from school to school. There wasn't much time for gossiping in school – other staff and the children hustled for your time (rather naturally!), but teachers made the most of their short coffee and tea breaks. The women, by and large, had blamed the "other woman" – a pert young blonde who was new to Julian's staff and "full of herself" and "what she wasn't going to do wasn't worth doing". Elaine must have watched as this much younger woman – full of the vibrancy and laughter of youth – had run off with her husband, while she managed the home and looked after the children.

Two years ago, she had faced the pain, heartache and embarrassment. Now, was she to face the blame, or would that fall on the shoulders of the young woman? *"My heart is broken, knowing that he was unhappy enough to do this"*: the words from the newspaper came back to Andrew.

He remembered feeling sorry for Elaine – not simply because her husband had left her, but more because she seemed a rather tender person. Andrew felt that she was easily bruised. Of course, he didn't know her: quite the reverse might be true when she was at home. Nevertheless, to be deserted and widowed in less than two years must be hard to bear by any standards other than those of the war zone.

The spaniel – a Cocker by breed and nature – was a good walker. As they approached the station, Andrew let her off the lead, knowing Mary would have 'gone mad'. Part of the joy of walking the dog alone – however irresponsibly – was that he could indulge in the kind of foolishness that wives find unbearable. Andrew felt that he and the dog had a good relationship; he just knew that she would stand by him. True to form, 'Lady' – his nickname for her: the family called her by the chosen name of Madge – kept close by his heels, as he walked up on to the platform by which the London-bound trains would stop. There he sat and watched the iron rails resting securely on their sleepers.

He found himself wondering whether it had just been some terrible accident, or whether Julian Price had intended to commit suicide. Why else, he thought, would a man with no apparent intention of catching a train, come to a quiet, country railway station? There was no bustle here – no urgency. There was no shunting of carriages, no clanking of chains and no hissing of air as the engine braked to a halt. Had he just come for the peace and the quiet?

The newspaper had mentioned 'Sunday night'. Had they meant 'evening'? What hour did he choose for his departure of this life? Julian must have come and waited. Did he wait for the dark and a passing train? Andrew supposed that there would have been no chance of the train stopping. Had it travelled fast or trundled by as did the heavy goods trains? Did he fall, or throw himself, in front of the train? Did he lie down on the tracks and wait? What a truly horrific wait that would be! 'The sound of a train striking a person is like the sound of a pumpkin being hit'. You might die in seconds if you were lucky, but if you were not what would happen to your body? Andrew visualised the broken bones and the amputated limbs – and closed his mind to every picture. What would drive a man to do that? The question would not go away.

"Where have you been?" questioned Mary, when he arrived home.

"I walked the dog in the park," he lied, as he removed his coat and hung up the lead. He found lying about such trivial things easier than telling the truth; the truth always led to so many questions to which he had no satisfactory answers.

"You might have said – I'd have come with you."

Andrew knew that this was not the case, but said nothing. His daughter, Amy, might have done, but she'd left early for university to be with her boyfriend. His younger son, Robert, would not have done – unless asked – because his nose was always into something new on the computer, and why shouldn't it be? His oldest son, Jonathan, would have come, whether he wanted to or not, if Mary had persisted. Andrew hadn't wanted anyone with him at all – either from a sense of duty or because they had been pressured to do so. He'd simply wanted a quiet walk with the dog. He wanted to get away from unanswerable questions – not a family safari.

"I don't understand you at all these days," insisted Mary.

Andrew often wondered what she meant by that remark, and pondered the question whether she – or, indeed, he – ever had understood.

Chapter 2

Role-play

Suddenly, everyone in the staffroom was an expert on suicide. Andrew had expected that, and he took his coffee to the far corner and sat quietly, listening to the flood of knowledge around him. One woman, in particular – a fat woman who was always cutting into other people's conversations between munching, benignly, on some cake or biscuit, sounded as though she might have written a text book on the subject. Her name was Elizabeth, but everyone called her Lizzie, which to Andrew seemed, somehow, inappropriate: he imagined 'Lizzies' as being on the thin side. She sat in the centre of the staffroom, holding court.

"It must have been awful," she said, relishing the sound of her voice, "You don't die quickly unless you're lucky enough to be decapitated. If the train just hits you a glancing blow, you could live on for hours. It might only break your spine and cripple you. You would be best to just lie down on the track, unless you timed it right and managed to throw yourself directly in front of the train as it passed the platform."

They were all dying to know how Julian had done it, of course, and could barely wait for the results of the inquest to be published.

"It could just lead to permanent brain damage. The best way is to …"

"Could we change the subject," interrupted Megan, the deputy head, who had noticed the distaste on the faces of some of the older staff.

"Well, it happened, didn't it? There's no good hiding away from the fact," said Lizzie with a shrug.

Her companions looked scandalised, and Megan passed across the room with her coffee and sat next to Andrew. The conversation broke up, and little islands of concern sprang up in the sea of chatter.

Andrew picked up snatches from a group of older women, most of whom were married and whose sympathies were with the wife.

"It's his wife I feel sorry for. How on earth is she going to tell her children?"

"They'd been together for twenty-three years when he left her."

"It was probably a guilty conscience."

"Surely, you don't do something like that because of a guilty conscience!"

"I've no sympathy with him at all. He should never have left his wife. She's a lovely woman …"

"… and their two children are delightful."

"Fancy leaving two young children? The little boy can't have been more than six when he went."

He sympathised with them. Here were views that held society together. The family unit was the centre of everything. They were right – Julian had no business leaving his wife and young children for a 'dolly bird'. He smiled, darkly, as the thought came into his head.

"His new partner is a lovely person. She's going to be devastated. They hadn't been together long."

"She had no right taking a man away from his family."

"Let her find a man of her own."

"Life isn't always that simple."

"She broke up a good marriage. We all have our ups and downs."

"If she hadn't been there – on his staff – simpering round him …"

"It was a love match made in Heaven."

"Don't be ridiculous – the little tart caught him when he was down."

Andrew noticed how the word 'tart' brought the conversation of each little island to a halt. One of the 'old boys' on the staff had butted in on the talk; his voice boomed from where he stood by the coffee machine. He smiled and continued, obviously intent on provoking a reaction.

"He was nice chap was Julian – played rugby at the weekends with one of my sons. He was under pressure at work, and Little Miss Love-match dropped her knickers at the right moment – or wrong moment! It depends how you look at it. Either way, it's a bloody shame. No man should be driven to what he did."

Jack Tate was a 'character' on the staff, and had become almost a parody of himself. Andrew was never sure whether he meant what he said, or whether it was merely for effect.

"When you find the right person – go for it! Nothing else matters. I wouldn't hesitate myself," said a very attractive woman, named Antonia. "If I met the love of my life, I'd just go. I couldn't bear not to be with him."

"You wouldn't leave your children?"

Antonia's eyebrows shot up. She pursed her lips and shrugged. It seemed obvious that she wouldn't have given the matter a second thought, but Andrew felt unable to believe that of any woman. His life was, perhaps, too narrow he thought. The people he had known were of a certain kind. Were there women out there – attractive and vibrant women – who, once they met such a man, would throw away everything for the love of him?

"Did you know Julian very well, Andrew?" asked Megan, softly, so as not to draw the attention of the other staff to her question.

"As a fellow head, but not socially."

"Was he under stress?"

"He ran what Ofsted describes as an 'outstanding school'. Can you imagine being outstanding *all the time?*"

"He had a high staff turnover."

"Doesn't that say it all? Last year, we received six thousand pages of guidance from the Department of Education – or whatever they've renamed it, these days – and I expect he read every word, as well as trying to hold down his job."

"And did it do the children and staff any good?" Megan responded, conspiratorially. She was a great comfort in the real world, and Andrew knew how much he owed to her support.

Back in his office, Andrew felt unable to concentrate on the papers before him. It was staff appraisal time. He laughed at the word 'appraisal'; it was so much more comforting than 'assessment', which implied that one was going to be judged. 'Appraisal' implied praise rather than judgment; it was typical of the soft, but tedious, approach favoured in education.

How would he appraise each member of his staff on the basis of what they had said about Julian Price? Were any of them speaking the truth as they actually felt it, or were they all just playing out a role? Had the role been self-imposed or allotted by the group?

Among the younger women, there had been a degree of contempt for Elaine Price – the contempt being focussed on the fact that she had 'been unable to keep her man'. The younger women, clearly, saw that they would have no difficulty in doing so when the time came. Andrew wondered whether they would be so confident, ten – or even five – years down the line.

The older women, conversely, saw no good in the 'other woman' at all. Whatever the faults in the marriage of Julian and Elaine, the other woman's intervention had caused nothing but harm to everyone. Left alone, the older couple might have made a go of it.

Jack Tate agreed with them and, in addition, seemed to find no fault in Julian. He was a man and a man was naturally 'red-blooded', and the young woman should have let well alone.

Andrew had no doubt that had it been the other way around, with Elaine leaving Julian, he would have been the butt of everyone's humour. Even in twenty-first century Britain the cuckold was a laughing stock – a man unable to satisfy his wife.

Would the women have excused Elaine? Would they have put it down to her being 'moody at the time', 'suffering from her nerves' or a 'victim of her monthlies'? He rather thought that they might.

Mingled with the contempt on both sides, however, there were shades of sympathy for the one betrayed. 'Anyone can make a mistake' seemed to be the general attitude, but not more than once. He didn't see any of his staff as having sympathy with the serial adulterer. People in his world allowed a degree of freedom for the errors of others, but freedom was always bound round with the conventions of the time. No one was ever totally free, and no one ever should be: even for the one error, there lingered, afterwards, a degree of contempt.

CHAPTER 3

Funeral

Andrew attended the funeral with Mary. Both had been able to arrange time off work – he as his own boss, and she as a good, hard-working and trusted member of staff – and they joined the mourners as the organ played. Andrew wondered why the little church opened its doors to them all – believer, agnostic and atheist. He wondered, also, what Julian's family and friends sought as they trooped, slid or marched in – confirmation, assurance or nothing at all?

He was attracted by country churchyards, without knowing why, and he was both overwhelmed and comforted by the sheer ritual of the church service. Once the 'happy-clappy' brigade took over in his local church, he had ceased to go to the morning service – not from a lack of faith (which he possessed only to a measured degree) but because the church no longer offered sanctuary or peacefulness.

Eyeing the graves as he passed along the path of tarmac and aggregate, Andrew felt no sense of fear with regard to his own death: his time would come when ... someone (?) ... was ready. He did feel that he would like to choose 'the manner of his going', as someone else had once said. He felt sure that when the time came – if it came in the natural course of events – his body and mind would know, and be prepared for the moment. This was such a peaceful spot; here, in this well-tended churchyard, was the final resting place of Julian's ancestors. Perhaps, at the end of the day, one couldn't hope for more than to be at peace in the shade of these trees and trust that, sometimes if not often, one of your family might come, sit upon the wooden bench and wonder what forces had shaped you.

He wasn't sure how prepared Julian had been. Was it true – as a priest had told him – that once their mind was settled and committed to the deed, suicides felt a sense of relief? In that final rush of the train, was Julian Price swept away to somewhere peaceful where the chains he had known in life were unshackled forever? Andrew hoped so: it was too awful to consider that at the end, at the moment the carriages rolled over him, he had wanted to get up and reach back for the platform.

The vicar talked of Julian's family. He spoke of how Julian had been "born and bred" in the village of Westerfield and how at the age of eighteen he had left Northgate Grammar School and gone to university where he had taken a degree in education. Julian had never wanted to be anything other than a teacher. At university, he had met Elaine and they had fallen in love, and remained in love ever since. When he obtained his degree, Julian "had no hesitation" in returning to Ipswich to teach. "What you take out of your community", he had once said, "you must put back in".

He spoke of the joy both Julian and Elaine had felt at the birth of their two children, Rosemary and Matthew, and how they had "struggled to run a good family home" while "holding down two extremely demanding jobs".

Julian had progressed rapidly from teacher to deputy head and then, finally, to headteacher – always teaching in or around the town he loved. To each school with which he was associated he had brought "commitment and enthusiasm". He was respected by all who knew him and worked with him – children, teachers, governors and parents.

His great enthusiasm had been all aspects of the "world of science" and he had "awoken children in his care to the excitement of science". The school's last Ofsted report had stated that Park Avenue Primary was "a flagship for the country when it came to science teaching".

Julian had, also, been a "formidable rugby player" – a quarter-back renowned for his "combative style" and "unbelievable sprint". His local club – for which he played at weekends – talked of his "commitment and passion".

As the vicar's voice rolled out the credits of someone who, by the accounts of all who spoke for him, had been a remarkable man and "good all-rounder", Andrew Mansell asked himself the question – why? This man had killed himself, leaving all those who had trusted, respected and loved him to live on, carrying the unbearable burdens of grief and guilt. There was no condemnation from anyone – only that profound sense of waste: a wasted life.

The vicar ended by saying that a book of condolence was open in the church, and the family would be pleased for Julian's friends to sign it.

When the coffin was carried from the church, it was the look in Elaine Price's eyes that held Andrew's attention. The widow – the estranged widow – looked up along the aisle as she processed with her children behind the shattered body of her ex-husband, and Andrew Mansell saw only a desperate pleading for understanding.

"He was so dedicated," said a councillor who Andrew remembered, vaguely, as being connected with the education service. "Naturally, we shall do all we can to support the school."

Andrew knew this to be true. Suffolk Education Authority had always had a caring – one might say, paternalistic – attitude towards its workforce. Yet, there was only so much that they could do. In the end, everyone would have to care for themselves and look into their own hearts and minds.

"It's distressing. I cannot say how distressing," said Julian's Chair of Governors to Andrew, "We are doing everything we can at this difficult time to support the school."

"Of course," Andrew replied, not knowing how else to respond but aware of his own inadequacy.

He had become separated from Mary as the mourners left the church and congregated in the churchyard. She arrived by his side and tugged at his arm.

"I told you not to leave me," she said, once the Chair of Governors had wandered off to commiserate with another group.

"I was collared by ..."

"I know – I saw, but I told you not to leave me. I don't know anyone here."

'It isn't a social,' he thought, but said nothing.

"Our condolences go out to the staff. How they will pick up the tools and get on with the job, I cannot imagine," said Mary, as they reached a group of

Andrew's fellow headteachers who stood back from the graveside, watching from a respectable distance.

"It's a time of adversity for everyone. I don't see how anyone could have done such a thing," replied one of the women, giving Andrew a hard look that he failed to understand. He could only assume that she supposed all men were capable of committing suicide, as it was supposed they were all capable of committing rape. Was it more common amng men? If so, he wondered why.

"I'm stunned. He was so well-liked by everyone, and he seemed to have everything going for him. A good school, a good staff, a good Ofsted ... "

The head's voice trailed off, and he made a gesture of resignation with his hands.

"What more could a man ask for?" Andrew replied, lamely. Mary 'looked daggers' at him, but she had misinterpreted his thoughts; the comment had not been intended as ironic.

"So sad ... so shocking ... "

Every group through which they drifted, as Andrew and Mary left the churchyard, expressed these thoughts. No one could understand what had driven him to that one, awful moment on the station. But perhaps that moment had begun long ago. Perhaps suicide started long before the final moment – rather as 'overnight success' took a long time coming?

"Stunned ... absolutely stunned ...he was so well-liked ... "

"It's a huge shock. He was such a good man to work with."

A group of Julian's own staff stood by the kissing gate, some trapped within its confines and others lolling

20

on either side. Huddled together, they were too distressed to watch by the graveside. All the women were crying, and most of the men had tears in their eyes.

"He was fun."

"He was full of life – so enthusiastic about everything he did …"

Amongst the group was a young woman – pert and blonde – and Andrew knew, instinctively, that this was the mistress or 'partner', which was the preferred terminology. He could see from Mary's face that she had made the same assumption, and the disapproval blazed from her eyes.

"We have to support each other," said one of the younger women to Andrew. It was Emily Saunders – Julian's deputy.

"Of course," he replied, squeezing her arm, gently.

"Did you know her?" questioned Mary, as they walked to their car.

"Who?"

"You know who I mean."

"I'm sorry."

"The woman who spoke to you – Julian's deputy."

"Oh, Emily? Yes – we meet at … you know …INSET sessions."

"It's Elaine I feel sorry for – Elaine and the children …"

"Julian was a loving father by all accounts.

"A loving what?"

"Do you fancy lunch at The Swan?" suggested Andrew.

"We've just been to a funeral!"

"We have to eat."

"Well let's find somewhere further from the church."

They finally ended up in their 'local', since it was the first pub they came to as Andrew drove into town.

"Do you really think Julian Price was a 'loving father'?"

"That is the received wisdom."

"It hardly ties in with him leaving his children and Elaine for that blonde!"

"No."

"You sound as though you approve of what he did."

"I don't really see much beyond the grief, at the moment."

"Elaine has been humiliated. I felt so sorry for her this morning. She didn't ask to be put into this position, did she?"

CHAPTER 4

'All happy families are alike ...'

It was the weekend, and Andrew Mansell was in the garden when Mary called from the kitchen door:

"You haven't forgotten Robert needs taking to Woodbridge, have you?"

He had, but then he'd been busy. During the working week, early mornings were always busy – with the dog to walk, the pets to feed and the breakfast to cook for the rest of the family – and, at the weekends, they were even busier.

They were lucky enough to have a large garden, which Andrew felt obliged to cultivate, and it was Saturday morning. He never cooked breakfast at the weekends, and so was able to make an early start in the garden. Once he'd fed Amy's rabbits and given them their weekly clean-out, Andrew had turned his attention to the vegetable plot. There was much to do. The potatoes, carrots and beet needed lifting and if he didn't harvest the apples, which they were lucky to have in the orchard, the birds and bugs would have them. There were also crops to plant for next year – lettuces, cauliflower, spring onions and broad beans (Mary's favourite).

He looked around him and saw the flower borders also awaiting his care. Mary looked after these when she had time, but autumn seemed to get busier for her as the years went on, and he knew that she had her church stall at the autumn fair to organise. Clearing the foliage from the perennials could wait but, if they were to have a colourful showing of spring flowers, the bulbs needed planting now.

"He needs to go, Andy!"

Andrew walked back over the lawn. It was sad at this time of the year. He needed to aerate, spike and scarify it before applying a dressing of compost. In case he'd forgotten, Mary had reminded him during the week. The man at the paper shop told her that he had just done his own grass, which always looked really healthy.

"I don't know how I'm going to get all this done," fretted Mary, as he kicked off his boots and walked into the kitchen, "I can't let the vicar down."

"No, of course not," he replied.

"What do mean by 'of course not'?"

"Of course you can't let the vicar down."

"You sounded as though you were being sarky."

Mary was slicing scraps of pastry from the crust of an apple pie she was about to put in the oven when Robert sloped into the kitchen. The surfaces of the kitchen units were littered with baking powder, eggs, nuts, packets of fruit, bags of sugar, scales, measuring jugs and the other accoutrements of cooking.

"I'll just help myself to some cereal," said Mary's twenty-year old, a week away from starting his third year of a four-year university course.

"I thought you had to go to Woodbridge?" insisted Mary.

"There's no rush. I'm just going to take a look at Chas's new computer game."

"In that case, would anyone like a cup of tea while Rob eats his cornflakes," asked Andrew.

"Not now, Andy – you can see I'm busy."

"I'll wait in the car," said Andrew.

"There's no need to be like that."

"I won't be in your way, then."

Andrew did a lot of his thinking in the car, driving one or other of his three children somewhere – music lessons, school plays, football games, sleepovers. With the youngest on her way to university, all that was going to end. No one would be more pleased than Andrew, who had often found that he was driving in three different directions at once.

As he drove along the A12, annoyed at having nearly lost his temper, he realised that he had never really considered, to any extent, Mary's virtues: like most husbands he took them for granted. Yet he would have been the first to acknowledge that they were the bedrock of their family life.

He remembered the moment he first became aware of Mary when they were at university. A stooped figure, over-laden with books and files, had scurried past him in the corridor. She had been close on the arm of her friend. Women always had friends, he noticed, and they clung to each other – like shipwrecked sailors, adrift on the sea of life, clung to a spar. He wasn't sure whether that image was from that time, or whether it came later: either way, he was aware that it was pretentious, but he kept it to himself and offended no one. He didn't mind female friendships, but wondered why they were so intense – and why, once a man had appeared on the scene, they were so ... dispensable. Was that true? If it was, was it best left unsaid?

He recalled an overwhelming desire to put his arms round her shoulders and tell her that "everything would be all right", and that "there was no need to worry". He had wanted to do that – had wanted to be of some use to someone. Since then, he had seemed to spend his whole life reassuring Mary to no avail because he was never able to offer enough comfort and certainty.

He had never asked himself what attracted him to his wife. He had put the attraction down to 'love' – that overwhelming feeling that here was someone who was special to him, someone for whom he would have done great things and given his life, if necessary. He never doubted this, or asked why it was so.

Their relationship had not been easy at the start. One of his friends had actually commented on their "tremendous clash of personalities", but he had put this down to his friend's cynical attitude to women and ignored it accordingly. However, despite their heated discussions, there had been an underlying love and trust.

They'd had much in common. They both enjoyed literature and spent hours discussing books. A particular favourite of Mary's had been Jane Austen and her "sublime irony". He had read the first sentence of *Pride and Prejudice*, and then put the book down on the basis that anyone with that view of life must be trite and not worth reading. Andrew preferred D H Lawrence, but Mary had only read the early books and despised Miriam for some reason that Andrew could never understand. Later, he felt that there was something of Miriam in Mary. Perhaps that had been the reason for her dislike, but he was a young man in those days and was not to know.

They both had a religious sense. He had appreciated his church school education and – armed securely with a background in his faith – was in the early stages of atheism. Mary had no religious experience at all, but a deep longing for understanding and reassurance. Not having been baptised, she felt vulnerable. Andrew led her back to the church he had left.

She was 'open' with him, and talked of her childhood and upbringing; she brought to the surface family matters that had been dormant for years. He had reciprocated, and so trust had been borne, one to the other. They came to know each other and each other's families.

They had travelled together as students, and worrying about these things had taken a back seat to their joy in each other's company. She had delighted him with her knowledge of France and its language, and his confidence in her had ignited her confidence in herself. Mary had blossomed when they were together.

Little gifts had passed between them – not gifts that strained the pocket or sent one running to the bank, but thoughtful gifts: gifts which said 'he or she has taken an interest in what I like or do'. Later, these gifts became part of the home they created.

Mary's unacknowledged virtues: had he really been unaware of them?

Once they settled down to marriage, their desire for a peaceful home had dominated. Neither of them had wanted their children brought up within the hearing of arguments. They had both wanted a home – a real home, a place of peace and quiet that was clean and welcoming and where everyone could 'flop out'; and he and Mary had worked hard to create that space for their family. The cost had been not so much in money as in time and effort.

The children had cemented their marriage, and the 'family years' had been happy ones. Indeed, his second child, Robert, had written them a letter, when he'd gone to university, thanking them both for his childhood. 'I couldn't have had a better one,' the boy had written, and Andrew kept the letter in the drawer of his desk. He had been grateful for that letter; it had been his 'spar on the sea of life'.

The children had come rapidly, each following fast upon the heels of the other, and they had been close – the two boys, Jonathan and Robert, doting on the younger, the eagerly-awaited girl, Amy. Close in age, yet so different in temperament – and that had been one of the delights: that they had reared three distinctive individuals.

They were a close family – everyone said so; most of their time had been spent in each other's company, and their children's friends were always welcome. There were never any arguments in the home and – with the odd exception of Mary's brushing up against her oldest son from time to time over what he wore – never any dissension. Amy had once said to him "It's good being part of a family that enjoys being together". Andrew had never asked her what she meant by that, assuming she would tell him if she needed to do so. He imagined that it had something to do with her boyfriend's family who were what is described as 'dysfunctional' – an unpleasant euphemism for the old-fashioned 'broken'.

Mary was a good and caring cook and they always sat down to meals as a family – every evening, without fail – and listened to each other as they shared, or didn't share, the day – each according to their natures. Jonathan, the companionable one, always provoked. Robert, the quiet one, always chuckled. Amy, the thoughtful one, always listened. There was a rivalry between the children, but it was always amicable – each seeing the faults of their siblings in a way that was not apparent to the parents.

Mary's unacknowledged virtues were her love and trust, her wide-ranging intellect, her conscientiousness, her vulnerability, her sense that there was more to life than the living of it, her openness, her enthusiasms, her little tokens of love, her care for their family, her love of their home ...

Andrew was aware of these, but wondered whether he'd treasured them enough.

CHAPTER 5

Invitation to dinner

A fortnight had passed since the suicide of Julian Price, when Andrew bumped into Elaine at a meeting where their respective schools were to discuss how they might improve their early years' education along the lines recently proposed by the government. Since Andrew considered his school boasted one of the best nurseries in the county, and since the previous government proposals had only been made six months before, he couldn't quite see the point of the meeting. Judging from the tired faces around him, he supposed that nobody else could either, but it was good to talk.

His surprise at seeing Elaine raised a smile from her as he entered the room, and after the meeting had fizzled out an hour later he walked with her to the car.

"Surprised to see me back at work? You have an expressive face, Andrew."

"Yes, I was surprised. To ask a silly question – how are you coping?"

"It's better to be at work – and, besides, Julian left us two years ago. I can't begin to consider that he is no longer in the world – that will come later – but I have grown used to not seeing him around the house."

"And the children?"

"Very quiet. We sit together in the evenings. Sometimes we talk and sometimes we ... just share each other's company ... It was a relief when the inquest was over ..."

"Yes, I can imagine."

"The coroner concluded that he did intend to take his own life."

"Had you ever doubted that?"

"No."

"They do say that ...," Andrew began, intending to offer the possible consolation that suicides are said to find a certain peace once the decision has been made. He wasn't sure that he believed the truism and couldn't imagine reaching the point where he might consider ending his life.

"I know but ..." interrupted Elaine, "the man he was has been lost to us for a long time."

"I'm sorry, Elaine."

"I thought I was ready to talk, but I'm not – not yet. Everyone at school has been very kind. It's all cuddles and comfort and quiet offers to listen, and the head's been wonderful – "Come in if you want to, but we'll have something in place if you don't" ... I think Julian understood what he was doing. Anyway, that's what the coroner said. I must go now. The children will be waiting for their tea."

"You're late," said Mary, "Did you remember that Jonathan needs taking to his big band practice?"

"No – can't he have the car?"

"I need the car. You'll have to drop him off and bring it back."

"And how will he get home?"

"If you drop me off at the WI, you can have it to pick Jonathan up later."

"Will you be able to get a lift home, or shall I pick you up?"

"Well, you don't mind, do you?"

How could he mind? Andrew, Mary and their two sons were sitting down to the evening meal. The oldest boy, Jonathan, had completed his university course, obtaining an honours degree in mathematics, and was considering "taking a year out". Andrew had been under the impression that this meant working for charity, but apparently it could also mean sitting around to recover from the strain of three years at university. Having been a teacher for over a quarter of a century (and having never had the chance of a "year out") he couldn't quite grasp why it was necessary or why Mary seemed eager to support the idea.

"Everyone does it these days, dad," offered Jonathan by way of explanation, as he shovelled back his mother's excellent beef in stout with dumplings that she had served with horseradish mash and glazed carrots.

It was certainly true that Mary's older sister's daughter had done so; the girl had back-packed around France and ended up picking grapes.

"So what are you going to do with the year?" Andrew asked.

"Well, you know – chill out and stuff."

Robert laughed, reading his father's mind and forestalling any comment. Andrew glanced at him across the table and smiled. In all honesty, it was a smile he did not feel whole-heartedly.

"And you have remembered that Robert goes back to Newcastle, next weekend?" asked Mary.

"Yes, I have as a matter of fact. I take it that we're going up on Saturday?"

"Not we – you! We've got that dinner party in the evening."

"We're entertaining the same weekend we're taking Rob back to university?"

"No, we're invited out. I promised Mona I'd do the table centrepiece for her, and I have to get ready."

"It's going to be a bit of a dash, isn't it?"

"Not if you leave early enough. Rob's happy to make an early start, aren't you?"

"Sure, mum – no problem."

It was at least a six hour drive to Newcastle, and another six back. Andrew made a quick calculation that if they left at four in the morning he could take a two-hour rest break and be back by six o'clock in the evening. This would give him time to shower and change, and he said as much.

"We're due at Mona's by 7.30 so you'll have to make sure you are back by six. I don't want you falling asleep in company."

The boys laughed: Andrew's propensity for 'dropping off' was a family joke.

He enjoyed the drive to Newcastle, refused a beer but accepted a bacon sandwich, crashed out on his son's bed for an hour and then drove home. He'd always got on rather well with his sons by the simple expedient of "leaving them alone to get on with it". This wasn't a policy that appealed to Mary, but they agreed to differ. His daughter he had circled warily, knowing that women see things differently and not wanting to fall out with her; Mary felt that he was "shirking his responsibilities".

He realised how tired he was when he got out of the car. Facing a shower and a shave seemed an awful burden at that moment. Andrew hoped that the Dawson's boiler might have burst, and that the dinner party had been cancelled. Immediately, he trembled with the thought that, if this were true, the dinner might have been relocated at their house.

Mary was ready when he walked through the door, and dashing around looking for wire to fasten a bouquet of autumn fruits and foliage that she was to take as a gift. Mary was very good at flower arranging, and Andrew could not but help admire the bouquet, which was unusual and would certainly be unique.

"Where have you hidden the wire? I always kept it in the kitchen drawer. How can I be expected ... Was Rob alright? Did he arrive safely?" she cried, shaking with dual concern for her son and her bouquet.

"Rob's fine. He was arranging to meet some friends at their local, when I left. The wire is in the shed. I was using it at the weekend to ..."

"Well, can you get it? I can't go out there in this dress. You should have put it back where you found it, and then I wouldn't have to ask. You'll have to be quick in the shower. We have to be there in an hour."

"I'm sure Dennis and Mona won't mind if we're a few minutes late."

"Late! We can't be late. It would be rude. Can you get that wire?"

Andrew had not been looking forward to the dinner party. On the way back from Newcastle, he had hoped, quietly, that the car would break down and delay him. It didn't have to be an expensive breakdown – just something minor that he could use as an excuse for not arriving on time. He had a vision of himself arriving home to a nearly empty house – only Jonathan would be there – and sitting down with his son and a peaceful whisky.

The Dawsons were not a couple he liked. It would be one of those occasions where the men stood talking in one part of the room – or even a different room – and the women in another. The men's chat would be all hearty or, worse still, matey, bristling with clichés about women, money and sport. The evening might actually end in a game of cards – more exactly, two games – because the Dawsons played bridge. Andrew did not like card players to any extent, and had a particular dislike of bridge players. He had been brought up on card playing as a social activity where the emphasis was on participating rather than winning; it hadn't been a world where you got truculent with your partner because they had "played the wrong card".

Mona Dawson was a good cook and the meal was excellent. She served melon and tomato soup, pointing out that "the tomatoes were ripe", wondering whether "the taste of basil was apparent" and pretending to worry that it might not be. Andrew was not sure how she would have survived the evening had her guests been unaware of the basil. This was followed by blackened chicken, served with aubergines, corn cobs and baked potatoes. The dessert was baked orange tart. The meal was mouth-watering, and Andrew could only admire her skill.

He was something of a cook himself, having produced three of the week's evening meals since his wife returned to work some years before. He had, also, always cooked breakfast for as long as he could remember – even before his wife returned to work – to avoid the morning hysteria when Mary tried to do five jobs at once. She had found it impossible to get up, iron the children's clothes, get them to dress, cook the breakfast and pack their lunches ready for school – all at the same time. Andrew had pointed out that she could have done the ironing the day before and put some of the packed lunches into their boxes. Since the children actually dressed themselves, and could be relied upon to wash themselves and clean their teeth, this only left her having to get up and cook the breakfast, while he got ready for work. This suggestion didn't go down too well, and neither did his comments about the myth of women and multi-tasking, and so he took over the breakfasts, leaving Mary to flap about.

Easing back from Mona's table he congratulated her, and could only admire the way she had provided a meal which would "put the women's minds at rest over putting on weight, while still giving the men something to get their teeth into".

The rest of the evening went as Andrew expected with the one-upmanship he had feared to the fore.

Mary had primed him to realise that Shaun Nesbitt was a successful dentist, and explained how he purchased old houses and had a builder he knew "bring them up to scratch" as residential homes for the elderly. He had several in different parts of the town and they were "filling a desperate social need". Andrew wondered whether old Victorian houses were the best accommodation for elderly people, but his comment was not well-received.

She also pointed out that Gilbert Rouse was a wealthy builder who bought derelict land and built schools, hospitals and sheltered accommodation for the elderly. Andrew couldn't quite see what was so good about this, and wondered why the council had to pay over the odds for a piece of land that Gilbert got for next to nothing. He couldn't quite see what was so clever about swindling the local taxpayers.

Dennis, she had already told him, was a helicopter pilot who flew crews out to the rigs, and "was making money hand over fist". Since Mary had never been particularly materialistic, Andrew wondered why she was impressed by Dennis's earning power.

Gilbert commanded great admiration by explaining how he had bought a piece of farmland for next to nothing from "an old boy who didn't have an eye for its value", and persuaded the council that it was the ideal site for a new school. It had taken a lot of "wheeler-dealing" with councillors but, in the end, he had got the contract and "made a bomb".

The conversation went quiet when Andrew questioned the decision to site the school next to a busy roundabout, and Mary caught his eye.

He was almost asleep before the bridge games started and began to scream quietly to himself when the bidding commenced. The language was combative and almost judicial – 'bonuses awarded', 'penalties for failure', 'extreme caution' were terms he had read in a book Mary gave him so that he "wouldn't embarrass her next time".

Dennis was sure that "a skilful player never failed to make a contract". Somehow – Andrew thought – this seemed to remove the fun from the game. Gilbert threw his cards down before one game had been completed, saying that he "conceded to Dennis's skilful bidding". Mona simpered that "Dennis could tell what every other player had in their hands".

As the bids, passes, doubles and redoubles whirled around the table, Andrew's head nodded forward.

"I don't know what got into you! I can't take you anywhere these days," said Mary, when they arrived home, "These are our friends. I don't know what Mona thought. She must have worked all day preparing that meal ..."

"Just over an hour."

"What? How do you know?"

"She'd have made the soup and the tarts yesterday, and I asked her for the chicken recipe," replied Andrew, thinking that he had worked harder driving to Newcastle and back.

"Is that what you were doing in the kitchen?"

"Yes."

"I suppose she thinks you do all the cooking in the house. People must think I do nothing. You're undermining me, Andrew."

CHAPTER 6

The other cheek

Meeting Elaine Price in town on that Saturday morning was the purest twist of fate, Andrew thought to himself, later. Mary was busy in school and she had needed "one or two things which I won't have time to pick up, so can you get them for me if you're going into town?" He hadn't been going into town – he still had much to do in the garden with logs to chop and store ready for the winter fires – but Andrew decided that it might be a good idea to make the trip.

It was an easy walk, and he enjoyed the autumn stroll across Christchurch Park. The beech leaves had fallen, and Andrew noticed a squirrel digging among them for the nuts. Overhead, swallows gathered for their flight south. He paused for a while and looked at the spread of trees that surrounded the pond. He was particularly fond of the silver birch whose white trunk and fresh spring leaves had a beauty all their own. His grandfather, during one of their Sunday morning walks, had told him that the birch lived anything up to two hundred years. "Give them plenty of light, and they'll stand up to frost and sun alike," the old man had said.

He walked down Northgate Street, past the library where he had spent so many hours as a youth, and bumped into Elaine on the White Horse corner, by the hotel made famous by Dickens. Her face lit up when she saw him, and he knew she wanted to talk.

"How's the term going?" he asked, somewhat fatuously but knowing that it would get the conversation on the move.

Elaine laughed, ignored the question, told him that she was shopping for the children while her mother looked after them and asked him what he was doing. Andrew told her that he was after some craft items for Mary, and Elaine smiled at him again. He knew she was thinking that no one had shopped for her for at least two years.

"Do you fancy a coffee?" he said, not knowing why he asked, but Elaine smiled a "yes" and he led her back up Northgate Street and along Tower Ramparts to the new Wetherspoons.

After a few preliminary comments about Mr Pickwick and the lady in curlers, and what Dickens would make of the White Horse becoming a Starbucks, Elaine began to talk. They knew each other only professionally, and Andrew realised that he was the virtual stranger to whom she could speak. A sense of guilt had set in, which Elaine needed to explain, and a face was better than facebook.

"... He had been suffering from so much stress. He left us – me and the children – over two years ago, you know, but I don't think he's been happy since ... I tried to stop loving him, but I couldn't ... in some ways, I blamed myself for him leaving. I wondered whether I had driven him out. You know what teaching is like. I would come home and go on and on about the day I'd had. Sometimes, I saw his eyes glaze over as he listened, and I knew he couldn't take much more – he had his own day gnawing away at him – but I couldn't stop. I just had to talk to someone ... but I wonder, now ... Sometimes, I would still be going on about work when we went to bed. It wasn't conducive to ..."

"Yes," said Andrew, reluctantly, "It's much the same with Mary and me. The off-loading begins over the dinner table, and continues throughout the evening. I don't think you're unique in that, Elaine."

"I don't see how the new relationship helped ... I don't think he was any happier. In fact, I know he missed the children – if not me ... My love for him hasn't ever gone, really ... You don't actually stop loving someone, do you?"

A young waitress placed their order before them – two coffees, one black and the other white, and a piece of carrot cake for Andrew.

"I wish I'd had a piece, now," laughed Elaine, and Andrew ordered another slice as she protested that she was on a diet. He couldn't think why, but nearly every woman he knew seemed to be on more or less permanent diets.

"He came back, briefly, soon after he left, but it didn't work. It wasn't what I thought it was going to be. I thought that I'd be ... forgiving him, but he seemed ... arrogant about what had happened ... and then left again, abruptly. Is it always hard to forgive? I thought I could forgive him. My love for him has never gone ..."

Elaine paused, and stirred her coffee. Andrew, his mind trying to handle an emotional situation about which he had no direct experience, remained silent and waited for her to continue.

"He had broken my heart, but I wanted to forgive him – I really did. It's hard to explain your feelings at such a time. I hated her, but couldn't blame him somehow ... Perhaps it would have been easier if I could have done ... I never started divorce proceedings, you know – and Julian never asked me to, which was strange. I felt I couldn't divorce him – not with the children so young ... In a selfish way, I'm rather glad now. It sounds better to be a widow than a divorcee ..."

Andrew had never failed to wonder at the way women looked at life; he felt it must surely be his male ignorance that prevented him seeing the difference.

"You felt the children wouldn't want you to divorce him?"

"Yes – in a way. Whatever Julian had done, he was their dad ... and they loved him."

"Did they choose to live with you?"

"Yes – right from the beginning. Julian saw them every other weekend, but they didn't want to be in the house with her."

"No, I can understand that ... From his point of view, Julian must have found that difficult."

"It was his choice to go ..." replied Elaine, her voice hard-edged and almost savage. She looked across at Andrew, before continuing "... He wanted to be with the children – I know that. Despite what he did, he loved them. It was hard for him – just seeing them every other weekend ... He wouldn't come into the house. He just sat in the car waiting for them to come out."

"He saw them every other weekend?"

"Yes – otherwise, I wouldn't have had a weekend with them. I'd have been the one who did all the weekday

2

stuff – running them round to their clubs, seeing they got their homework done, getting them off to school."

They drank their coffee and ate their carrot cake, Elaine asking Andrew if he could finish her piece because it was too much. He smiled and took the cake from her almost without thinking about it: such was the power of custom and habit. Andrew was very still as a person – something which irritated his wife for reasons he had never understood. Mary always said that the dog – her dog – liked him best because he was so still. It was like that now, and Andrew knew that his quietness was drawing Elaine on to speak.

"I suffered – especially at first. I confess that I was driven by a hatred of her and him for what they had done to our family. We were a happy family, Andrew, before she came along. He loved the children – he was always doing something with them. I loved him, then."

"And still do?"

"Yes ... I can't come to terms with his death. I can't accept that he was unhappy enough to do what he did."

"How have the children taken it?"

"You mean have I told them?"

"Yes."

"I thought it best. Education is a small world, and the news was all over town. I didn't want them to hear it in the playground."

"No, of course not. I think you were right."

Years before, when a suicide had occurred in their family Andrew had kept it from his own children. He had often wondered, since, whether that had been the right decision.

"I talked it over with the Reverend Stiles," explained Elaine, "and he seemed to think it best. He said that children come to terms with things in their own way."

"Did they blame you?"

"All they ever wanted was for us to be together. Rosemary exploded at the beginning – you know what girls are like – but she's been most supportive since. It's Matthew who cries now. He's only nine – little more than a baby, really – and I still put him to bed. When I tuck him in – something his daddy used to do – the tears just roll down his cheeks, night after night. He doesn't say anything. He doesn't have to – those tears just tear me apart ... After they're spent, he'll cling to me, as though he's afraid I'll go, too. When he's asleep, I climb into bed, pull the duvet up round my ears and howl. Nobody really understands, Andrew, the pain of a broken home. It's been like that – on and off – since Julian left ... I'm sorry ... my friends and my family have tried to help, but no one really understands ..."

The tears were rolling down Elaine's cheeks, and she looked up at him as though he were the only one who could get her out of what was now an embarrassing situation. He placed a tenner on the table, secured it with a coffee cup and led her out onto the street. No one noticed as they left, but that wasn't the way Elaine saw it.

He led her up Northgate Street, intending to walk her on to the park – Andrew could think of nowhere else that might offer some privacy – but, as they reached the library, Elaine released her arm and turned to him.

"I'm sorry ..."

"There's no need to apologise. You obviously had to get out of there, and this seemed the only way to go."

"I'm OK now," she said, abruptly, "I'll be OK. I have to finish the shopping, anyway. Thank you, Andrew."

Elaine turned and walked away down the street. He couldn't understand her sudden, almost brusque, departure. One moment, she seemed to need him ... and the next, he was an obvious embarrassment. When she reached White Horse corner, Elaine disappeared into the crowd of eager, Saturday morning shoppers.

Andrew continued walking towards the park, and then realised that he had come into town for those things on the list that Mary had left. He was annoyed – with Mary, with himself and – strangely – with Elaine. Where the hell was that craft shop? He turned again and followed Elaine's trail into the town.

With the needles and silks in a small brown bag, Andrew felt calmer and made his way home. The woman in the craft shop had been most helpful, laughed at the hopelessness of men and found Mary's things for him. He was now only angry at himself for being angry, and he laughed.

Standing by the duck pond on the park, Andrew wondered. What are men looking for in marriage? It was generally accepted that men are more satisfied and happier with their marriages. He'd read that somewhere. It was also accepted that women play a major role in creating a happy and positive atmosphere in the home – that they create the home, in fact. Was that true? Was either of these truisms actually true? Men like a comfortable home – both emotionally and physically, and value a woman who can create this. He couldn't dispute that – not in his case, anyway. If these assumptions were true, where had Elaine gone wrong? Was she too demanding or too dominant? What kind of woman was Julian looking for when he left his family? How important a part did the home play – did peace at home play – in Julian's decision to leave it? What had made him, supposedly, both unhappy and unsatisfied in his marriage?

On the pond, a pair of mallards was being chased by two rogue males. On the whole, though, it was a simple life being a duck. As the cold weather approached, one felt sorry for them, knowing that they were stuck on a cold pond, while a roaring fire waited at home. Mary had often said that, as they stood watching the ducks scudding across the surface after the crumbs she had thrown. How many people did he know who longed for the simple life of the duck?

He had been confused for a while – confused by the collision of emotions that Elaine's sorrow had stirred within him – but he had gained control of himself, now, and he would be calm, and ready to face 'the faces that you meet'. Eliot had said something like that in one of his depressing poems – poems Andrew had admired as a young man.

Holding the bags carefully, he made for home.

CHAPTER 7

Snap?

Mary was waiting for him when he arrived home.

"Where have you been? You've been a long time," she said, as Andrew handed her the bag of craft items.

"I thought you were busy in school."

"We finished earlier than we expected. Sue said we'd done quite enough to please the Ofsted inspectors. Where have you been?"

"What were you doing?" asked Andrew, eager to avoid her question.

"There was a bare patch of ground by the pond. Sue thought it would look better planted out."

"You've been planting shrubs!"

Andrew couldn't help saying it. Planting was something in which Mary never got involved. Somehow, he couldn't picture her with a spade. He, also, couldn't help wondering whether it mattered.

"It gives the right impression when they arrive."

"How many of you does it take to plant a few shrubs?"

"I might have guessed you would say that!"

"The inspectors might do better just looking through the children's work."

"Oh well, of course, your school is wonderful, isn't it? We all know that."

"Do a few shrubs make the difference between 'good' and 'outstanding'? If they do, they shouldn't – and I can think of better ways to spend a Saturday morning."

"She's asked us if we'll go in tomorrow, too – there's a lot of work that needs triple mounting."

Andrew relinquished the argument; pursuing it could cause an ill feeling that would permeate the weekend. Mary, also eager to change the subject, asked him what he wanted for dinner, but nothing was further from his mind. A quiet anger, for which he did not wish to find words, engulfed him. She sensed this, and he knew it.

"Where have you been?" she asked for the third time.

"I only needed to get your craft items," he replied.

"You've been a long time. I expected to find you here when I got back."

"I met Elaine Price in town. We had a coffee."

"Oh?"

"She had a lot to talk about."

"Your place is here with your family – not drinking coffee with a work colleague."

Andrew looked at Mary with astonishment. He saw clearly her suspicions, yet he had never so much as nurtured any desire to be unfaithful. He considered the remark both unjustified and hurtful. He had never given her any grounds for doubt, and she had no right to make such assumptions about him.

"You might have been seen," she added, as though aware of his feelings and wishing to alleviate the scorn in her comment.

"We had one coffee and a piece of carrot cake at Wetherspoons," he said, "I can see no harm in that."

"Hmm – very nice."

He couldn't see or feel that he had done anything to warrant the sharpness in her voice or the twisting of her mouth. Angry beyond any kind of reason, Andrew went into the kitchen to make a cup of coffee.

By dinner time, the matter was forgotten – at least, Andrew felt that Mary had forgotten it, but it gnawed away at his heart. Mary, full of the Ofsted inspection that was imminent, talked incessantly about it. Talking about her work was something Mary never ceased from doing and, over the years, Andrew had come to accept it. His mother had once told him that their daughter, Amy, had commented to her that "Mum wouldn't be able to do her job, if it wasn't for dad. She asks his advice on everything." It had brought Andrew much comfort to know that his daughter was aware of this.

"Are you listening to me," asked Mary, "I feel I'm talking to myself sometimes."

They had sat down for the meal at seven, and it was now nine o'clock. They had talked through the government's u-turns, the umpteenth scaling down of the national curriculum, the managerial bureaucracy surrounding every area of school life and the mountain of paperwork it involved, how education standards were best gauged, whether those who issued guidelines actually understood how children learned, the pace of change, how teachers were to achieve a better balance between local diversity and nationally approved standards …

"I don't think we should be in this state just a few weeks into term, do you? I feel trapped in a vicious circle.

I'm conscientious. I'm a good teacher. I'm popular with both staff and children. Usually the beginning of term is fine and I can switch off, but this year the stress response button is continually on and there's no time to relax – no time for an evening out. School work just takes over your life and conversation. I don't feel I've got any resources left to cope. I'm forever saying 'I haven't got time' ... This is when stress becomes really dangerous, you know. You need to make time for yourself and restock the exhausted system ..."

Andrew wasn't unsympathetic – he was, after all, in the same boat himself – but he couldn't see the point of talking about the problems, endlessly. It ruined their meal, it ruined their evening – and it solved nothing. 'It's good to talk'; was ever a bigger lie perpetrated on a gullible public? No, it wasn't good to talk; it was good to sit quietly, and let all the rubbish flow out of you like so many toxins.

"Oh well, if you can't be bothered to listen! If I can't talk to my husband, who can I talk to?"

Yes – but your husband is also a human being, not a receptacle for verbal garbage – not, in fact, a bin for all the words wasted in the education service. "Just focus on the job – you and your class of children; everything else is just so much detritus". How many times had he said it? How many times had he tried to talk her down? He even said things he didn't actually believe in order to calm her – everything else clearly wasn't 'detritus', but it did need to be put into perspective; so many of his colleagues – his wife, more to the point – took everything on board as though the gods had spoken. It was as though the trillions of words that poured from the Department of Education (Andrew insisted on retaining that nomenclature – changing the title didn't change the purpose) were the elixir of life or manna from Heaven.

It wasn't until their sons arrived home at ten o'clock that Mary stopped talking, and it wasn't until they sat in bed together that she, once again, asked about Elaine Price.

"How is she, then?"

"Wondering why it happened … blaming herself."

"It's a bit late for that, isn't it?"

"How do you mean?"

"Well, she needed to sort out that little hussy who stole her husband, long ago. If she'd done that, this may never have happened."

There was a perceptiveness about women that always amazed Andrew, and was one of the reasons why he valued their conversation. It was as though they shared an understanding of the deeper things in life. More than that, they seemed to have a collective intelligence. It wasn't the first time he had heard Elaine blamed for "losing" her husband, and listened to what the speaker would have done about it "if she had been in her place." Those he had heard express opinions were also sure it wouldn't have happened to them.

He hoped Mary – and the others – were not right, but had this awful feeling that their quick assumptions might prove correct. It seemed to him to be a betrayal of the complexity of human nature to suppose that any motivation could have been that simple, and with such awful consequences.

Even if they were right, however, did they dig deep enough into the male psyche? Did any of them ask why Julian had left Elaine in the first place, or was the reason assumed to be merely sexual? Was that true? Were men as "simple" as women liked to suppose? Quick as they were to reach assumptions, did any of them really know why many men behave as they do – and all at about the same time in their lives? Women were perceptive about human relationships in a way that men were not – no one could convince him otherwise – but they were also prone to accepting 'pat' answers – the received wisdom of the moment. Currently, discussion of the 'male menopause' was much in vogue, but Andrew wasn't convinced that such a thing existed – not, anyway, as it was perceived.

"You're quiet," said Mary.

"I was just thinking."

"About what?"

"About what you just said …," he replied, knowing it to be flattering, even if untrue. "Why do you suppose that Julian's affair was the reason for his suicide, or that Elaine could have prevented it?"

"Well, he broke his marriage vows, didn't he – going off with another woman. If he was the wonderful man they all claim, he can't have felt good about that …"

"There's more than one way of breaking your marriage vows," replied Andrew.

"What do you mean?"

"It's all about 'love' and 'honouring', isn't it? Sexual betrayal is just one aspect of those promises. There are other ways of being un-loving and dishonouring your husband or wife."

"What do you mean? I hope you're not suggesting that I am like that!"

"Like what?"

"Like you've just said – that I don't love or honour you."

"I didn't say that."

"You implied it."

Yes, he had, but didn't want to pursue it now. This was the moment to retreat before an argument broke out between them – one of those quiet, hissing arguments carried on behind the door so that the children wouldn't hear. It had simply occurred to Andrew that talking to your husband or wife as though they were something the cat had dropped off didn't show much love or honour.

CHAPTER 8

Moving on

The gossip surrounding Julian's suicide burned out as quickly as it had flared up. As the schools made their way towards half-term, other concerns engulfed them, and everyone wanted to "draw a line under it and move on". Nothing was to be gained by continually "going over old ground". Such, thought Andrew to himself, is the way we value the past – no wonder we never learn.

Clodagh was one of those bombastic teachers – a know-all of the first water. Her view was generally the only view worth considering; all other views were trodden underfoot, as she made her way through classrooms, schools and professional development centres. She was physically big, too; indeed, Andrew wouldn't have flinched at describing her as fat. Clodagh could not fail to fill any staffroom with her presence and her opinions. Andrew was glad that she wasn't on his staff, but valued her as a supply teacher. She exuded efficiency and expertise: any class of children were safe with her for the day, should their own teacher be absent for any reason.

Flitting from school to school, and never taking on more work than was viable for tax purposes, she came new to all situations. It was Clodagh who resurrected the subject of Elaine and Julian.

"It's time for her to move on," she boomed, joyfully, "at least she's a widow and not a divorcee. She can be thankful for that – she's entitled to her death-in-service benefits, and quite right, too."

Jack Tate laughed and egged her on by wondering whether "Little Miss Love-match would be entitled to her share."

"I should think she's had her 'share', as you put it, Jack. No – the wife gets it and deserves it. Marriage is one long sacrifice for most women. The least they deserve is to be looked after if their husband deserts them, although it doesn't work out like that unless you're careful."

There was a ferocity in Clodagh that Andrew could not place; as far as he knew, she had been married to the same man, Peter, all her life – a man who did just about everything that needed doing. She'd helped at one of Andrew's summer fairs, once – running a home-produce stall – and her husband had stood dutifully by her side all afternoon, except when he'd been required to fetch and carry, or erect and dismantle the stall; but, then, perhaps you could never tell. Each marriage makes its own rules.

At the end of the day, he went to thank her for coming in at short notice (he'd had to phone her, rather desperately, at 7.30 that morning) and asked if she could also do the following day. It was during this conversation that the subject of Elaine and Julian came up again.

"She never did get on with his people, you know. You can't afford to fall out with your in-laws. You can say what you like to your husband – after all, you're married to him – but never insult his mother or father."

"Why didn't they get on?" asked Andrew, timidly, as though Clodagh would have expected him to know that, or – at least – have the savvy to work it out.

"Does any wife get on with her mother-in-law? Not usually, do they? But, I think, this was a particularly bitter disagreement. Julian's parents live near me, and so I've only got one side of it, but they weren't very cooperative about baby-sitting – took the line that they'd raised their children and Elaine ought to do likewise and not expect to be out and about as though she was single. I think the old girl stuck her nose in once too often, as well. Advice is one thing – interference is another."

"You think that's why Julian left her?"

"It might well be one reason – it's what his mother thought. She said he'd had enough of her going on about his parents. Well, you can see his point, can't you? Would you like to listen to someone running down your mother and father day after day? I know Elaine has come out of this smelling of roses – betrayed and now bereaved – but it wasn't all one-sided."

"Did his parents see much of Julian and his new partner?"

"They were often round – took to her like a duck to water. She was a nice girl, by all accounts. Mind you, I think Jack Tate got it right – she knew when to drop her knickers," exploded Clodagh, roaring with laughter at her own remark, "Anyway, what's your interest in all this, Andy – just being nosey like the rest of us?"

"I know Elaine – vaguely – and I felt sorry for her."

"Oh – well don't believe all I say. I'm just passing on what I've been told."

"It has the ring of truth about it, though, doesn't it?"

"In what way?"

"What you were saying about Elaine not getting on with his parents. It can't have been easy for him. It would affect all sorts of things – such as how often the grandparents saw the children, and how easy the contact was – that sort of thing."

"Well, that's another thing, of course. The children adored Julian, by all accounts. He was all over them when he was with Elaine – took them everywhere. He was the one who did all the driving round – clubs, parties and activities – and, of course, he was mad about the natural world, and the children were like him. Really up for anything that involved being out in the fresh air – long walks and weekends on his allotment."

"And did they take to his new partner?"

"Well of course they did!" retorted Clodagh, "She was young and lively, and took them to Macdonald's for happy meals! When Julian got the chance to see them – every other weekend."

"You sound as though you're on Julian's side in this."

"Do I? Well, men do those kinds of things, don't they? It's no use pretending that you are a nice sex, Andy. It's up to the wife to keep her husband in line – to set the ground rules when you first get married."

"No chance of Peter getting out of line, then?" laughed Andrew.

"I'd nail his balls to a tree. When you get married, your wife and children come first – accept it, or don't get married. Peter and I got things sorted out *before* we got married and brought children into the world. His first duty is to me and them. What he might want comes second. I don't blame Julian, because you men are weak and it was up to Elaine to trim his sails."

Andrew sighed as he slipped out of the french windows, signalled the dog to be quiet, made his way down the garden, and so across the road and onto the park. He had tried to sit and think in his study, but Mary had wondered why he "wanted to be alone in there" and her concern for his welfare drove him from the house. It was always quiet in the park – if rather chilly as autumn wore on – but he did much of his thinking there, away from the demands of the house and family.

Why did women always complain that it was cold? "I'm cold." How many times had he heard that bleat? Why didn't they simply switch on, or switch up, the heating? Was there some need to let you know that you had allowed the house – and hence them – to get cold? Would Clodagh have told Peter that she was cold – Clodagh the independent, iron-willed lady – or would she have flipped the switch herself? Andrew didn't know the answer to that question. The older he got, the less he seemed to understand women.

Clodagh didn't blame Julian, simply because she assumed all men were weak and had to be controlled; but there was no admiration for their better qualities, either. Did she look upon her husband like that or was it just other men? Did she and Peter live an harmonious life because he knew his place in the pecking order? And how did Peter look upon all this – was he content with his lot?

Conversely (or was it similarly?) Clodagh blamed Elaine for letting the marriage fall apart, yet that was clearly not the case. Julian had been driven by other forces than his wife's dislike of his family. There was, for example, her constant harping on about her work. Did Clodagh talk endlessly about her school day when she arrived home, or did they have rules about that, too. Yes – they probably did, but who made them, and to whom did they apply?

Andrew took the dog's ball from his pocket, flung it as far as he could and watched Madge run after it. How many times – foolishly – had he and Mary wished for their lives to be as simple as their dog's? It wasn't that they argued much, but when they did it was bitter – as though grievances had been stored for the right moment. Was it better to "have things out"? You couldn't deny the sense of that, but not over and over again – surely?

Would he have been happier with someone like Clodagh – someone who demarcated his place in the world quite clearly? No – no, he most certainly would not, but it would make life simpler, wouldn't it?

As these thoughts drifted, somewhat aimlessly, through his mind, Andrew Mansell was aware that none of them were high upon his agenda of concerns at that moment. Clodagh's comments about Elaine not getting on with Julian's family were what troubled him most. He had never got on with his own parents particularly well – especially his father – but, at the same time, he did object to Mary's dismissive attitude towards them. He must take some blame for that, of course, but, even so, it didn't excuse Mary making remarks like "If you're not careful, you'll end up like your father!" or "You wouldn't expect your mother to understand. She's always been a cold person. 'Stoical' is the word for her!"

Was there something wrong with being stoical? Surely that was better than complaining all the while? Come to think of it, he'd never heard his mother complain. Madge barked at him and he threw the ball for the umpteenth time.

CHAPTER 9

The diary

The package – unopened by his secretary because it was marked 'Private and confidential' – was waiting with the other mail, when Andrew returned from his drama lesson with the early years children. He'd enjoyed his morning; maintaining a 40% teaching timetable, since he had taken over the large primary school in Ipswich, was the one thing that kept him sane and interested in the job of teaching.

If it hadn't been for this, he would have been crushed under the avalanche of advice and guidance on how he could do his job better, which arrived each week from the Department: guidance issued, of course, by people who had never actually done the job. What an easy target education was, he thought, for every government to single out for improvements. Probably 94% of schools were doing a good job, and so politicians could always claim success whether they'd accomplished anything or not. They'd have been better employed focussing on those schools that desperately needed help, but then failure would stare them in the face. Much easier to tell those doing well what to do!

He scooped *Art and Music at Key Stage 4, Additional Advice to the Secretary of State on Art, Music and*

Physical Education at Key Stage 3, *Careers Education and Guidance* and *Education for Citizenship* into the rubbish bin, and placed those papers relevant to his teachers ready for the Friday notice-board displays. He then picked up the brown paper parcel and opened it. Inside was what looked to Andrew like a diary, as he flicked through the pages, rapidly. Enclosed with it was a letter.

Dear Mr Mansell,

I hope you'll excuse my sending you this diary, which belonged to Julian, but I didn't know what else to do with it. I'd no idea he kept one until I had to sort through his things. I haven't read it, I might add.

It goes back several years, long before he and I got together, and I thought it should be returned to his wife, but didn't like to just post it to her. I was told that you and she are friends, and hoped that you might be able to get it to her.

I can't just throw it out and I can't keep it, so I didn't know what else to do with it. I hope you don't mind, but if you do then you'll just have to send it back.

Thank you for your help,

Yours truly,
Jodie Smith

Andrew didn't like to read it either but wanted to – or, at least, wanted to flick through the pages and have a quick glance at what Julian had written. He was bemused. The letter didn't sound as though it came from a mistress; the tone didn't suggest Jack Tate's "Little Miss Love-match". Was 'Jodie Smith' the kind of name you associated with a mistress? How was he supposed to approach Elaine Price? Why was his name linked with hers by someone who knew Jodie Smith? Had Jodie Smith read it? Were her motives as straightforward as they sounded?

It was lunch time, he was at work and he would be needed in the dining hall. Diaries could wait: Andrew re-wrapped the book, and pushed it into his briefcase.

It was three days before both he and Elaine were able to meet in town after school, despite Andrew being clear on the telephone about his receipt of the diary. They strolled along the Buttermarket to the little café called Blends, and sat opposite each other at one of the little wooden tables, having ordered tea and scones, while Elaine read the letter.

"Why do you think she sent it?" queried Elaine.

"What else could she do?"

"Keep it."

"It contains Julian's thoughts over several years – before her time. Perhaps she thought you should have it?"

"Does it have entries during the time he was with her?"

"I haven't looked, Elaine."

"Do you think she has?"

Andrew couldn't imagine any woman not having done so – or, at least, not having had a cursory glance. On the other hand, was this Jodie worried that she might read things about herself that she'd rather not see? The natural curiosity – or simple nosiness, if you like – of women couldn't be disregarded: on the other hand ...?

"I don't know," he replied, diplomatically, "she says not."

He didn't like to add that he believed the young woman; he didn't want to set Elaine off on a diatribe against the girl. Why did men of his age always think of young woman as 'girls'? The expression had come, unbidden, into his mind.

"I don't know that I can read it either, Andrew. I don't know if I want to."

"Wrap it up and put it away for a while. Only be sure that it is destroyed before your children might come across it – unless you know what's in it by then."

"You think I'll read it, don't you?"

"Yes," he laughed.

"You might be wrong. I don't want to be hurt again. I've been through all that. I can do without finding things out that I'd rather not know."

"Yes, and I imagine that the young woman felt the same," he added, by way of what he thought was some kind of reassurance.

"Do you really think that?"

"I think it likely, and yet how can you destroy someone's memories? I think that's why she passed it on."

"Would you read it, Andrew – or, at least, skim through it to see if it contains anything which might be hurtful?"

He knew she was going to ask him that favour. Who else could she ask? She would know then whether to destroy it or not, without having had to suffer what it might say.

"You want me to know these things?"

"You're a man. You might understand the thoughts of another man. You and Julian must be similar in many ways – and, yes, I trust you to keep what you read to yourself."

"But I will know what you might prefer I didn't know."

"I'll have to take that risk, but I don't think so. Julian wouldn't have opened himself up in the way you suggest he might have done – not even in a diary. He wasn't that sort of man ... I can't just destroy it. At the same time, I'm not prepared to expose myself to what he might have to say ... You can filter out the bad bits for me," Elaine laughed.

Andrew felt flattered that she trusted him to such an extent; he didn't think he'd been trusted so fully since he was a child, and his parents had 'trusted' him. It was a big part of his upbringing – to be 'trusted', but how many wives actually trusted their husbands to do something as simple as washing the car or cleaning out the rabbits without plaguing them with advice?

Andrew waited until his wife had gone to bed before he crept into his study, took the diary from his briefcase, unwrapped it carefully, replaced the brown paper in his case and sat down to read Julian's diary. Only his eldest son, Jonathan, who was out with a friend discussing what they might do in their gap year (or not do, according to how you viewed the situation), might disturb him now – Mary was a heavy sleeper.

He felt uneasy about what he was about to do – much more so than when he had agreed to read it for Elaine's sake. There were some things you didn't like to pry into, but the words might actually bring some comfort to Elaine and even her children. He could understand why she wanted it read.

The entries were spasmodic. Some days they were written at great length, and then, on others, there would be nothing at all. None of them were ordinary accounts of day to day events; in each case, there was an edge to the writing – as though Julian had needed to get something off his chest. The diary covered many years and one entry – the first at which Andrew paused – had been written in 2005: this was at least three years before Julian left his family. His children would have been ten and five.

October 10:

I didn't want to come home tonight. I parked the car off the road and wandered across the heath, heading for The Garland. I just needed a drink. Then I changed my mind and went back to the car and drove to The Garland. We never go there. It's out of the way and quiet. I didn't want a lot of questions when I got in, and driving would save me time. It's bad when you need a drink to face the wife and kids, but I did. I do! These days I often need a drink to go home.

Elaine's got her monthlies and it's always the same when I get home. Nothing's right. Everything's wrong. And at the end of a day's work it's more than you can take, sometimes.

I sat in the pub for a long time and drank too much. I'd no choice but to drive back. I explained to Elaine that I'd had a drink with a colleague after work. She was none too pleased. The dinner was on the table and Rosemary needed taking to her dance class.

It has not been a good night. I might just as well have soaked it up before dinner. Once the children were in bed, she went on for hours – snapping at me in that voice she has once a month about everything from the fact that Matthew's CD plug needs a new fuse (and she asked me to do it days ago) to the fact that the driveway is covered with weeds. I really don't want to write anymore

... I can't talk to anyone without seeming to betray Elaine and I don't want to do that. If I did say anything, no one would understand, anyway.

The entry tailed off and Andrew closed the book. It was more than he could bear to read it. This was intrusive, and he would have to tell Elaine that he felt it wasn't right. The best thing to do with a diary like this was to burn it; the pain it would cause was unacceptable. Besides, Julian had used it as a confessional and never intended it to be read.

However, he did return to it – night after night and entry after entry: a little at a time, and then several pages together. The diary was the voice of a man who needed to be heard, and there had been no one to listen. It was a voice from the grave now, of course, but it had reached a sympathetic ear.

On the first occasion he returned to Julian's diary – two nights after he had locked it into one of his desk drawers – Andrew came across the following entry.

June 15:

Arrived at school today, and Tucker said, when I bumped into him in the corridor, "I've never seen anyone look as unhappy as you, Julian, when you arrive in the morning. You look as though you've got the weight of the world on your shoulders." He added, by way of a salve, I suppose, "You seem to cheer up during the day. Perhaps you enjoy your work more than most of us." He laughed, then, but no one enjoys his work more than Tucker so his remark came across as somewhat disingenuous, and his initial comment stuck in my mind all day.

Elaine and I had had a set-to when I left. Even as I tried to kiss her goodbye, her mouth was nagging on about something I hadn't done or needed to do. The grass needed cutting, I think. We've got friends round at the weekend for a barbecue. Her nagging never stops at the issue of the moment. She always brings up a dozen or more other things I haven't done – not within the last week, but ranging back over the years.

Andrew – shaken by what he'd read – closed the book and then, within seconds, opened it again, seeking the next entry. The diary had been left for some weeks, however, and the next entry was dated

August 25:

I didn't want to come back, but I am here and I had best get on with it. I long for term to start again. Life is so much easier when … when we are not at each other's beck and call. I really do feel like a servant, sometimes.

The holiday was dreadful. Holidays are dreadful. I had looked up what I thought might interest Elaine and the children and had planned the days accordingly. Then we got a long spiel about my not being "spontaneous enough. Why can't we just get in the car and drive somewhere?" When we did, of course, we ended up going nowhere.

A few days later, Julian had written:

August 28:

There is never complete disagreement between us, but there is never complete harmony either. I am uncertain about how she will react, and Elaine says the same about me.

Yesterday, we had a row about something and I cannot remember what it was – only the bitterness that followed. (Fortunately, the children were all out at the time.) It was hot, of course. It has been very hot since we returned from France and that hasn't helped. A lot of the

shrubs we planted in spring have died while we were away and, somehow, that's my fault. "Most men", I'm told, would know that planting should be done in the autumn but I won't be told, will I? But then, I'm not most men, am I? I don't put up shelves when asked, I don't repair CD players promptly, I don't ever listen (except that I hear her voice going on for hours), I don't seem to want to go out with our friends anymore, I used to be reliable ... It goes on and on, doesn't it?

Andrew began to feel as a biographer must: reading private letters, diaries and memoirs in order to build up a complete picture of someone who everyone may have thought they knew. He remembered some of the comments when the news of Julian's death had reached the newspapers: "a larger-than-life character", "full of fun", "a wonderful man", "an inspiration to his staff", "vibrant", "well-liked", "determined" ... and so the list went on.

This wasn't the man coming across in the diary. Andrew felt profoundly sad that Julian's friends, family and colleagues knew so little about him ... and yet they did, didn't they? To them he was the man they described, so tearfully, when the news of his suicide broke.

Another entry – earlier than those he had read, previously – said:

March 17:

Elaine doesn't seem to like the house, anymore. Yet we've put so much into it – in time, effort and money. She's harping on, again, about moving. Thinks we need a detached property. Her sister had just moved to a bungalow at Grundisburgh, and we never stop hearing about it. It makes you wonder whether it's worthwhile doing anything to make the place nice. What's the point if you're going to have to start all that slog over again somewhere else?

The Easter holidays that followed this entry were clearly a time of considerable tension. Andrew read on:

March 24:

We are constantly irritated with each other, and it's hard to put your finger on why or where the dispute starts. Elaine feels that I do not love her as I used to. She feels that she can no longer rely on me as she once did. It's not that she suspects me of seeing anyone else – which I'm not – but that I do not give her enough attention.

Once the rows start, all our differences come pouring out. I spend too much time on my hobbies, and the children suffer (despite the fact that they attend at least one club or take part in at least one activity every day). I insist on living in the town when everyone else is moving into the country. I spend too much time at my school. I make no attempt to understand her predicament (whatever this might be – it seems to change by the day, but somehow concerns whether or not she should go for promotion). "It's all right for me" – whatever "it" may be!

March 25:

They are moments of tenderness between us but they lead to nothing – they bring no lasting joy or harmony. That word – 'harmony'! It's what I thought marriage would be about – not this constant striving for something just out of reach but an abiding harmony between two people who loved each other.

March 27:

I sit here trying to trace back to where the argument started. I'm picking through the row in all its detail, and yet I cannot find where it began. There were the unpleasant exchanges, but it hadn't begun with anything about which we disagreed. Rosemary wanted a 'Staffy' – all her friends (or so we're told) have a Staffordshire bull terrier – and Rosemary wanted one. Both Elaine and I agree that it is out of the question. There was no argument there. We both agreed that Topsy, our spaniel, the two rabbits, the three Guinea pigs and the two cats are quite enough. We both agreed that the children – despite their original assurances to the contrary – do nothing to look after them (at least, not without a lot of persuading) and that the job of doing that falls on my shoulders. That was it, wasn't it – 'falls on my shoulders' – that was the remark which sparked everything off, despite the fact that Elaine agreed with me!

How did it go then? Did I expect her to clean out the pets as well as run the house and do a full time job and take the children everywhere because I was always at my school making it the best in the county?

But she doesn't run the house – I do my share. She doesn't take the children everywhere – I do that, usually. And no – I don't expect her to do a full-time job – I'm happy for us to live on my salary. I would prefer us to live on my salary and then I wouldn't have to keep listening to how difficult her job is, and carry the rap for the faults of all her work colleagues! It's Elaine who wants the career.

Why shouldn't women have a career? Men have it all their own way! Do we – what do I have all my own way? I spend too much time on my hobbies. OK, I like natural science: it interests me and it interests the children and, no, I'm not trying to exclude her – she can come on the hikes if she likes – yes, they do take up a long time – and yes, she does have time – no one asks her to spend hours at the weekends on housework – after all, we do have a cleaner!

Yes, sometimes I do need to shut myself away. I need a bit of peace and quiet. Yes, I do listen to her. I spend at least two hours every evening – if I'm not taking the children somewhere – listening to how her day has gone. But I'm not listening? What am I doing then? I'm sitting there, soaking it all up. Why do I do that, if I'm not listening? It's not for fun – it's not to keep my hearing exercised! Oh, so I don't like listening to her, then.

"Most normal husbands listen to their wives". How I hate those words – "most" and "normal". They are thrown, of course, as deliberate insults. Why? Why is it necessary to suggest that a husband is not like most men, and is not normal? Why do women suppose that they have the right to hurl insults in that way – as though verbal abuse is quite acceptable?

Julian seemed to have exhausted himself at that point because the entry went no further. He hadn't gone on to say how the quarrel had upset them both – and Andrew knew that it would have done just that; he hadn't gone on to say how they would have wanted to find peace together, and wished that they could erase the argument from their lives; he hadn't gone on to say how they would have wanted to show that they understood the other's predicament; he didn't go on to say that Elaine would have said, yes, she did trust him and she did love him and she didn't know what had come over her; he didn't go on to say how he would have apologised; he didn't go on to say, how they would have found that quiet moment together.

The next day, Andrew bought a lockable document case. He put the diary in it, locked the case and placed it – temporarily – in the lockable drawer of his desk. He would phone Elaine and, when she was able to meet him, he would return the diary in the document case, and advise her to keep it locked until such time as she might want to read it – many years from now – or might feel able to destroy it, utterly.

CHAPTER 10

Idle chatter

Andrew was more than surprised when Mary told him that she had bumped into Elaine, but he was – on reflection – unsure why: it was just that, somehow, he couldn't picture the two of them together, talking.

They had met in town, and "had coffee together", Mary had remarked. She added, rather smugly, that they "had gone to Pickwick's – not Wetherspoons". Andrew found himself wondering whether the coffee was any better, and supposed that it must have been.

Over a long evening, as the conversation drifted about between them, he learned that the two women had found "a lot of common ground". They both deplored the modern attitude to divorce, which had been one reason why Elaine had never attempted to secure one. "Not," she had confirmed, "that Julian had ever asked".

"He didn't seem to want one," pursued Mary, "which makes you wonder how serious he was about his new 'partner'."

Mary managed to invest the word with the same degree of contempt she might have reserved for 'social security scroungers' or 'sewerage'.

"Mind you," she continued, "I wouldn't have tolerated what Elaine did. I would have made him suffer. Men these days think they can have it all their own way."

Andrew wondered to which men she was referring; he couldn't think of any one of their friends who fell into that category. Most of the men he and Elaine knew kept quiet to keep the peace. Only Dennis Dawson put his foot down with any degree of firmness, and he was generally considered to be "a moody bugger".

"I think Elaine was quite a 'looker' when she was younger," Mary went on to say, "As you get older you lose those, and that's something that a decent husband would accept. He didn't have to pursue his dolly bird … You're quiet – what are you thinking?"

Andrew realised that Mary wanted the reassurance that she hadn't lost her looks, and that he agreed Julian should not have pursued his dolly bird. He was quiet because he was not sure there was any real connection between the two things. He went over and put his arm round Mary.

"You haven't lost your looks," he said, "A woman's beauty changes with the years. It doesn't get worse – it becomes different. Men understand that: it's your sex – in the main – that is obsessed with appearance."

"I think she was rather wild, too. I think they had a good time."

"What makes you say that?"

"Some of the things Elaine said. They went on lots of holidays before the children came along. They weren't like us – they didn't marry young and have the children straight away. By all accounts, they were quite a good-looking couple. Julian had her picture painted – there aren't many husbands do that, are there? They went to Italy, France, Spain – all the florid countries – and drank and ate with the best of them. They lived quite a gypsy life for a while before they settled down."

Andrew felt a sense of loss, as he listened to his wife. In her tone, too, he felt he heard a grievance, and, in her eyes, he saw it rise to the surface.

"Would you like a cup of tea," he asked.

When he returned with the drinks, Mary was still consumed by Elaine's past.

"I think she was sought after – well-liked by everyone. I expect she was quite a catch in her day, but marriage takes its toll on all of us."

Andrew was tired of consoling his wife, and buoying her up. He said nothing, and Mary looked at him as though he had neglected her welfare. He wasn't sure how much of what she said was Elaine, and how much was down to Mary. He realised that he never thought much about his wife's looks, any more than he thought about his own. He realised, too, that he had never viewed Elaine as any more than a woman who shared the same profession. Before Mary spoke, he had not seen Julian and his wife riding with gypsies across the Camargue.

When he thought of Elaine at all it was as a rather tender person. She was softly spoken and gentle in her movements. Thinking about her, as he listened to his wife, Andrew recalled the lack of anxiety with which she had unlocked and opened her car door. Remembering her face, he saw the high cheek bones (which are never a disadvantage when it comes to looks) and her large eyes. A little smile had turned the corners of her mouth into an attractive curve. Had Julian ceased to value those things about his wife, or had he simply ceased to notice them – or were none of these speculations relevant to what happened between them?

"What are you thinking about?"

He hated that question. Apart from the fact that he was never sure once the thought had passed, Andrew felt the query to be intrusive. How awful it would be if we ever became telepathic as a species!

"Nothing," he lied because he couldn't begin to talk about it.

"You must have been thinking about something," persisted Mary.

"I was thinking about what you said. I can't quite recapture the thought. Are you telling me that Elaine felt Julian left her because she had lost her looks?"

"It's not just that! When you're bringing up children, running a home and trying to hold down a full-time job it's bound to take its toll. You lose your zest for living. Men don't seem to understand."

"You mean men don't lose their 'zest for living', too?"

He realised he shouldn't have said that as soon as the thought was spoken. He was about to receive a long diatribe about 'a woman's lot', and he'd heard it all before, so many times.

"You don't understand ...," Mary began.

Andrew sighed, inwardly: it was not good that she should hear him sigh. Once, in a kind of desperate attempt to save his sanity, he had noted down, over the period of a month, how many times he had been accused of not understanding his wife. It had totalled 207 times, and it had been a comfort to realise that not even he could have failed to 'understand' on so many occasions. It had been a comfort, but only a temporary one: when it happened the next time he just felt bitter, realising that no man could match up to expectation.

"You don't begin to understand," she repeated, "I come home at night absolutely shattered. Have you ever thought about what my day is like......?"

He had – his were very similar.

"... and when I get home, there are meals to cook and the house to clean ..."

He'd always been under the impression that he cooked all the breakfasts and half of the evening meals, but he might have been wrong about that or it might simply have gone unnoticed.

"... Oh, I know you help, but men have no idea. They never ... it's the little things that are missed ..."

Andrew recalled his brother-in-law's comment on one occasion. After he had spent the morning cleaning and dusting and ... whatever else needed to be done, his wife had observed that he'd missed the light-shades. She'd been busy at church organising the flower rota at the time. His brother-in-law had cleaned the house and prepared the lunch before getting out to the gardening that needed to be done.

"... I know I'm going on ...," continued Mary.

"I wonder if Elaine did," Andrew asked.

"All women do."

"Do they? I wonder why?"

"Julian wasn't up to much around the house. He was always out somewhere with the children. She told me that. She thought that it irritated the girlfriend, too – the fact that he'd always got his nose into some interest or other."

"Isn't that good?"

"What?"

"That he had interests that involved his children – I mean, from Elaine's point of view."

"We can't always be out enjoying ourselves, Andrew. Someone has to keep the home going ..."

"Yes – but it's not the woman, is it? Not these days ..."

The conversation went round in its usual circles, and Andrew agreed that Mary was right in her views; there seemed no other way to bring their discourse to a close. Reflecting on what they had said, later, he could not but think he had wasted his time 'doing his bit' for the past twenty-odd years.

Andrew Mansell was a brooder. He knew it, and accepted it with some relish. Once a thought had entered his head, it never left him. Years later, it would pop into his consciousness during another conversation and his mind would drift back along paths that had not been trodden for some time. Walking Madge 'round the block' after Mary had gone to bed, he had several strands of thought running through his head.

The image of Elaine with which Mary had returned was not a flattering one. She had cast her in the same mould as 'all women'. That seemed to satisfy Mary. There was sympathy in her words, but not in her tone. Her attitude seemed to be that since Elaine had a wild youth she must now pay the price – as though there was always a price to pay for enjoying yourself. She seemed to believe that if you married a man like Julian then you must expect him to behave badly with other women at some time or other. There was a sense, in her beliefs, that there was always a balance in life – happiness balanced against sadness, conflict against agreement.

Was love, then, to be weighed against hate? Was there no harmony that ran through all things? Was there a perception that no one could be continually happy – that nothing could be, more or less, perfect?

Women always seemed to have some built-in dissatisfaction – as though they could not be happy unless something was going wrong. They enjoyed a crisis: one might say that they could not live without one. Thinking over times at work when 'the shit hit the fan', he realised that the women enjoyed those times more than the men. Conversation was always particularly animated in the staffroom, voices were at full stretch and there was an air of excitement in the office.

This thought – that he had been striving to achieve a harmony that was not attainable – mingled with the idea that he had simply wasted his time for the best part of a quarter of a century. It haunted him.

His wife knew that he had done his fair share – probably more than his fair share – of what was necessary to create a home and rear three children, and yet she persisted in denying the fact. Why? There was a contrariness about women that both mystified and terrified him. Did it spring from fear, or from a need to dominate? He was reminded of Eliot's chilling line *'That is not it at all, that is not what I meant at all'*. He feared that, at the end of a lifetime, he might still not understand.

"I'll be late in this evening," said Mary, as they sat down to breakfast the following morning, "Sue wants us to discuss this new government white paper, *The Importance of Teaching*, and the meeting is likely to go on a long time. I can bring fish and chips in. I know it's my turn to cook."

"Relax," replied Andrew, quickly, realizing that he was on the verge of losing his temper at her suggestion. She knew – had known for over twenty years – that he made no fuss about cooking at any time; he never raised the question of whether it was 'his day' or not. Besides, now all three of their children were at university, cooking for two people who knew each other's tastes so well was simplicity itself. So why the fuss? Was it just another attempt to introduce some conflict? "I'll whip up some tuna steaks with olive mayonnaise and potato wedges, for when you get back. We can have that with some green beans. It'll be very nice. Give me a ring when you leave school, and it'll be ready."

He knew he was annoying her, but couldn't resist the temptation. He knew he was annoying her, and understood why, but couldn't accept that it should be so. She had no reason to be annoyed.

"Tuna steaks?" queried Mary, "I'm not sure I feel like tuna steaks."

"OK. Give me a ring when you decide what you want and I'll whip round to the shop and get it – but you'll have to give me time to cook it."

"What's wrong with you this morning?"

"Nothing."

"Well, it doesn't sound like nothing to me. You must have got out of bed on the wrong side."

"Perhaps I've got a busy day ahead," replied Andrew.

"I really could do without this tension at the breakfast table. I thought once the pressure of getting the children off to school was gone, we might be able to enjoy each other's company, peacefully, at breakfast time. It should be a quiet start to the day."

It was one of the things they had discussed, endlessly – the harmony between them once the hectic days of running the children around were over. Such a discussion often wound down one of their arguments; looking ahead to a calm and unruffled future was one of their safety valves. Yet, it had nothing to do with the children being independent; the children had never given them any trouble at breakfast time, or at any other time. Jonathan and Amy always arrived on time and ate with them; Robert always dashed down at the last minute, stuffed his breakfast between two rounds of bread and ran for the bus. It was one of the things they laughed about as a family.

Mary had once said that she got upset with him because she wanted everything to be perfect between them and it frightened her when things went wrong. One side of him could accept that as true, while the other side could not. Happiness ... peace ... contentment in each other's company was to be the cornerstone of their marriage.

They saw themselves and their children inhabiting an island surrounded by a protective sea. Beyond this tempers may flare and verbal battles may rage, but they were safe within their magic circle. They were, perhaps, never happier than when holidaying together – away from the rest of the world, safe within the family nest, wherever it might have been built that year.

They were perceived as a happy family – "close" was what other people called them – and they were: he knew that to be true. He could feel it in his bones; he did not need to be told. His daughter, Amy, had once written him a card saying that it was good to be part of a family that got on together. That was two of his children, then, who had thanked both him and Mary for their upbringing. What more did he want?

He wanted an end to this bickering. He wanted an end to this ... Andrew couldn't find the words. Well, he could but they were not precise enough to express his unhappiness.

Mary's desire for this contentment in each other was genuine. Andrew had no doubts about her sincerity, but he could not accept that her fear of losing it justified her railing at him once a month, every month for the past quarter of a century. Love, surely, was expressed in how you treated the other person; it had no place with the sharp tongue and the foul temper.

Chapter 11

The other woman

"I hope you didn't mind," said Jodie Smith, "I didn't know what else to do."

"Not at all," replied Andrew.

"What did you do with it?"

"I got in touch with Elaine, and she asked me to read it."

"Did you?"

"Some of it, but you were quite right. It was very personal in places, and I've sealed it up – for want of a better phrase – in a document case. If Elaine wants to read it later she can, but ..."

His voice tailed off to indicate that, perhaps, it would be better for Elaine not to do so. He was very aware that the young woman had sought him out. It wasn't difficult, in teaching circles, to find out who was on which course and turn up at the Professional Development Centre. What did they call it these days – Continuing Something or Other? He much preferred the simple Teacher's Centre, and wasn't prepared to go beyond PDC for the sake of quite unnecessary change.

"If you'll excuse the stupidity of the question, may I ask how you feel?" he said with what he hoped was a comforting smile.

"Awful – I blame myself entirely."

He knew that she wanted to talk to Elaine, and that he was merely a substitute – a mouthpiece who might pass it on. Guilt was everywhere in the young woman's face – in the drawn mouth, the downtrodden look, the lank hair, the bags under the eyes and the dry complexion. She might have always been so, of course, but that wasn't what Andrew believed. This young woman hadn't slept for a couple of months – not real sleep, not full and guiltless sleep. 'Sleep; sleep that knits up the ravelled sleeve of care.' Shakespeare knew what he was talking about.

"There's a pub," he suggested, "opposite the station. The Railway Tavern, I think it's called. I don't know what it like, but there is parking there."

Sitting with a beer (Andrew) and a cider (Jodie) in front of them, both felt awkward and, for a while they chatted, idly, around the course (which Andrew had run) and their day. The pub seemed grotty, and Andrew felt dirty and judged that the girl did, too.

"Perhaps this is not the best time," he said, eventually, "Perhaps it would be better to have a chat at another time."

"No, it's kind of you to even talk to me – and now we're here … My friends are all on my side and I have talked to them, and they have been most supportive …"

"… but friends always are, aren't they, and so it's not very helpful."

"You're right – it's not. No one says anything remotely critical. 'Miss Smith would like to thank all her family and friends for support at this time'. That's what they said at the inquest, didn't they? But it isn't true – well, it is – I don't want to appear ungrateful, but … I need someone … on the other side, if you like, to know that it wasn't what it appeared to be. I didn't seduce him. I didn't lead him astray. I didn't break up his home. Julian came to me."

She looked at Andrew as she spoke, and he thought he could understand what had been the attraction. Jodie Smith was so young and – under what, in his day, had been called an 'urchin cut' – she stared out at him with a large pair of blue eyes. The blonde hair framing the wan face didn't help, either. Here was a young woman who was so open to the world and, appearing vulnerable herself, would attract those similarly exposed. Julian would see her all day, since she worked at his school. He would pass her in the corridor and smile at her across the staffroom without thinking twice. Andrew could feel them being drawn together. Her haggard face became even more ghastly as she looked at him, appealing for his support.

"You want me to make this known – however obliquely."

"Someone said you had a funny way of putting things," she laughed, "I just want people to know. Julian was unhappy and, when he came to me, it all flooded out. I don't mean that he ran his wife down – he didn't. He just talked about how he felt without blaming anyone else for it."

Andrew felt that could not quite be true. How would you speak of your unhappiness without mentioning the cause of it? He said nothing, eager for Jodie Smith to say what she had to say. He was uncomfortable, and wished he hadn't allowed the young woman to put him in this position. Already, he had dropped the 'girl' when he thought of her; she was a 'young woman' now – less in need of comfort and protection.

"Do you know – before he said anything to me, before he even spoke to me – Julian drove to my street and sat there in his car? He told me that, much later – after we'd got to know each other. He said it lifted him out of his life just to be there – that he felt free. He would walk up and down and everything – common things like the children playing on the nearby field or a sparrow picking crumbs from the gutter – would seem fresh and bright. He felt joyful, he said, and the burdens weighing him down fell from his shoulders. He said "on the street where you live, the sun always shines – even when it's raining". He was very romantic, like that … Can you believe that?"

Andrew smiled, but didn't answer the question. A distant memory tugged at him from somewhere. He could imagine feeling like that, and an unbearable sadness engulfed him.

"Go on," he said.

"That was how we were, most of the time. We were content in each other's company … but Julian couldn't throw off the guilt. He knew what he had done. He had left his wife and children, and he couldn't forgive himself. I didn't encourage him to stay. He was free to go whenever he wanted …"

"You were together for two years?"

"Yes …"

"Is it true that you and he had ended your relationship?"

She looked at him before answering. It was a long, hard look as though she considered his question impertinent.

"Sort of … he was planning to move out – just for a while."

"Did …?"

"I ended it, if that's how you want to put it," she said, quickly – so quickly that it seemed to Andrew she was 'snapping his head off'.

He smiled to himself (careful that she should not notice), recalling that he had been told "all women snap". He believed it, but refused to accept the truth.

"It had nothing to do with Julian refusing to divorce his wife, if that's what you think … he had become more and more moody. He was almost morose at times and would sit for hours staring at the wall."

"He missed his children?" suggested Andrew.

"Yes."

"Is that why he never tried to divorce Elaine?"

"I don't know. I think there was more to it than that. As I said, I never asked him to divorce his wife."

"How did he react when you told him it was over?" enquired Andrew, surprised at his own temerity.

"It didn't happen in that way. I said, one morning, that he had to make a decision about what he wanted. Not for my sake – I was happy to go on as we were – but for his own. He couldn't go on living in two worlds … He was constantly coming and going between the two of us. I couldn't live like that, and I didn't think it was good for the children. We'd been together for two years. I said that they had to become part of our world, but his wife wouldn't hear of it. So, when he had the children, every other weekend, Julian just drove around with them – going nowhere. In the summer it was bad enough; in the winter it was awful. It came to the point where he was glad to take them home ... He had access rights, of course, but that didn't make any difference. *She* wasn't going to have *her* children get to know me, and that's all there was to it ... We couldn't go forward together, you see."

Andrew understood what Jodie Smith was saying but he couldn't see why the "two worlds" made so much difference. Surely, she had Julian for all but part of two days every other weekend? Couldn't they build a life on that basis?

"He wasn't with me, emotionally, even when he was there. I needed him to decide whether I was part of his life or not."

"Men can live in compartments, can't they?" Andrew suggested, trying to helpful by showing that he understood.

"So I'm told, but women can't."

"Did he just leave?"

"No, no. It wasn't like that. I didn't give him an ultimatum. I just said that he ought to sort things out for his own sake."

"But people thought ..."

"People talk. They put two and two together and made five. I don't know where the gossip came from. We were still living together when ... it happened. That very evening, we'd had a lovely meal together and Julian seemed happier with himself. In fact, he seemed very calm and collected. It was a nice evening, and we sat in the garden, sharing a bottle of white wine. He'd even cooked the meal. It was a pasta dish ... As we sat talking, he got up and said "I've just got to pop out for a while. I won't be long". I remember asking him if it had got to do with school and he said "Yes, in a way." That was the last I saw of him. The next thing I knew, the police were at the door ..."

"I can't imagine how that must have been."

"What haunts me is the thought that people think I drove him out. His wife takes shelter behind that – as though she had nothing to do with his death. But we were happy together. It wasn't me who drove him from his home and his children. It wasn't me who put him in the invidious position in which he found himself. She was using the children to prise us apart, and he couldn't ... he didn't want to make that choice. Julian was forced into a corner, and he saw no way of escape – no way forward for us."

"How were things at school? People must have noticed a strain between you."

"Julian was good at his job. He was very focussed, and I don't think his misery showed that much. Besides, as you know, schools aren't the social workplaces that outsiders think. Everyone is too busy. I don't think his feet touched the ground when he was at work. The outside world was cut off. The children take all your attention."

"Do you think you drove him to it?" suggested Andrew.

"Do you?" she replied, looking at him, snappishly.

He realised that she wanted his reassurance that it was not so; she wanted "the other side" to forgive her, and he was their representative.

"That isn't the point, is it?" he answered. "The point is – how do you feel about it?"

"I feel he took my concerns for him as an ultimatum, but I didn't mean them in that way."

"But you wanted him to come to a decision?"

"Yes."

"And he couldn't?"

"And so his 'invidious position' became worse?" she faltered.

"Yes."

"And so I must take my share of the blame?"

"He was a grown man. Once he had taken that 'decision' – and I use the word very loosely because I don't think he was in a state of mind to make a decision – it was his responsibility, and no one else's. That's what free will is all about. You take the decision – you're responsible. No, I don't think you should blame yourself, anymore than Elaine should blame herself."

"I suppose the lesson to be learned is that we should all be more careful when we make our choices – when we try to fulfil our desires – and think how they might impact on other people."

"He was very vulnerable – just as you are now. Go carefully – we don't want another tragedy on our hands."

"One of my friends said much the same thing."

"I've no monopoly on wisdom," laughed Andrew.

Watching the young woman get into her car and drive off, Andrew felt waves of exhaustion pour through him. Her last words to him had been "You will let people know, won't you?" She gave him a smile and a friendly wave, and he knew he had been of use to someone, but the effort had left him feeling washed out. He had tried to be honest with her, while – at the same time – easing her burden; but he wasn't sure that he was right, or that he understood what had happened, any better than Jodie Smith. All he did feel sure about was that Julian Price's suicide had, selfishly and tragically, touched so many lives. The pain for him might be over, but for others it had only just begun and would mar their lives for years to come.

Chapter 12

Dissatisfaction

"How can you be dissatisfied if you're happy?" asked Mary, when Andrew relayed to her the gist of his encounter with Jodie Smith.

"Are you referring to Jodie Smith, or to Elaine?" he asked, provocatively.

"Well, *her*, of course – *the other woman*. Elaine was happy enough until *she* took him away."

"We don't know that," insisted Andrew, "Clearly, Julian wasn't."

"He wasn't happy with his mistress, either, was he – or she with him? Some men are never content. He had everything going for him – a job he loved (by all accounts), a faithful wife, a lovely home and two beautiful children. What more could he want? What did he think he would find with this girl that he hadn't got with his wife?"

"I don't think he knew."

"Oh, for God's sake, Andrew – grow up! It's obvious what he saw in her ..."

"Is it?"

"Well, why do men usually leave their wives?"

"That's just the accepted truism. It doesn't mean that it's true."

Mary looked at him, with fear in her eyes, as he spoke, and the fear turned to anger in an instant. The idea that a man might leave his wife for anything other than sexual reasons left her terrified.

"God, you're deep, you are," she exploded.

"Still waters," he replied.

"Do you know, sometimes you send a chill right through me. Sometimes, these days, I don't even know what you're thinking."

He wondered whether she ever had, or whether he had ever understood her, but dismissed the thought almost as soon as it came; they had talked openly and endlessly for all of their lives. They must understand each other.

They sat quietly for some time, too frightened to speak, and when Mary did open her mouth, it was to divert the conversation.

"I take it she wasn't happy with him, either, or she wouldn't have issued the ultimatum?"

"I don't think it was an ultimatum ..."

"Oh, Andrew, of course it was! She was clearing the decks. She was tidying things up, ready for the future. She saw him as a good catch. She wanted him, and Elaine and the children were in the way. Women understand women. It's only men who get sentimental about them."

A little shiver of apprehension – what the French word 'frisson' sums up so well – ran through him when his wife spoke. Did all women, including her, have such a cut and dried attitude to relationships and marriage? Did the romance follow the decision that a man was 'a good catch', rather than precede it? He remembered 'falling in love', and everything else seemed to follow. He couldn't ever remember wondering whether or not Mary was 'a good catch'.

He recalled the exact moment when it had happened. It was as fresh in his mind, today, as it had always been. The world seemed to be sitting on her shoulders, and he had felt sorry for her. He remembered the green cardigan and the tartan skirt, and the way her shoulders were drawn up around her neck. He remembered the blonde hair piled high on her head as she turned and caught his eye. His heart had turned over in his chest; the sensation of that happening had been a physical one – as though the heart actually had leap-frogged itself. He recalled her blue-grey eyes and the rather harsh laugh she gave her friend. Afterwards, for the few years it took for their children to be conceived and born, while they were making love, he always saw her as she had been at that first moment, and feelings of tenderness overwhelmed him.

Mary had some work to do that evening, and Andrew was glad. Their conversation before dinner had disturbed him, and he had brooded on it throughout the meal, which Mary had cooked. It had been one of his favourite meals – griddled steak with Dijon new potatoes, and Mary had served it with lightly steamed Savoy cabbage tossed in butter. Throughout the meal, he was aware that his brooding annoyed his wife, but he couldn't get a thought out of his mind.

He had once heard a woman say that "love changed over the years", but she had come from Eastern Europe, married her husband to gain British citizenship and was preparing to dump him. It had suited her to believe that, and Andrew dismissed it accordingly. He didn't believe that 'love changed'; he believed that love remained as it had felt in those first moments. You either had the feeling that this person was special in a way that other people were not, or you didn't: there was no room for change.

What he did believe, however, was that love needed to be nurtured. It could grow or be destroyed, but it couldn't be taken for granted. It couldn't be subjected to regular abuse and remain intact; if you loved someone, then that love was revealed in the way you spoke to them, and of them, and in the things you did for them. Love was not dismissive; love was uplifting. Love was about the way you treated each other every day.

He went to his study and closed the door behind him. Now that the children were all at university, there was little chance that he would be disturbed. His study doubled as a games room and they had a slate-bed snooker table down the centre, but no one, now, would come in for a game or to borrow a book. He took a novel from the shelf, and sat down. He opened the book – one of those sour stories by Kingsley Amis – and placed it on his legs, which were stretched out and resting on the desk. Andrew wasn't going to read, but wanted to give a false appearance. In that way, if Mary did come in, she wouldn't ask him what he was thinking.

His mind roamed back over their life together (or tried to) but returned quickly to those things about Mary which annoyed him. She had a habit of putting him in the wrong – quite unnecessarily. One occasion he recalled vividly was when Jonathan had returned, unexpectedly, one Friday night from university; he had been chasing after some girl or other and was taking her to see some pop group at the Regent. At breakfast, on the

Saturday morning, Andrew had set just two places – one for him and the other for Mary. (Amy, who was still at home at the time, never got up for breakfast.) Jonathan had arrived at the table while they were eating, and Mary had supposed that he'd been upset "because Andrew hadn't set a place for him". Why? What had led Mary to make any such supposition? It was quite unusual for Jonathan to be up for breakfast, and no one was likely to be less offended. So why had Mary said that – why had she felt the need to put him down?

They were entering the 'Festive Season'. It deserved capital letters when one thought about it, and deserved to be expressed in coloured lights – let alone inverted commas. It was the time for dining out, and inviting others back. Would your menu of chicken liver parfait followed by pan-fried sea bass, and rounded off with Turkish delight ice-cream be any match for the Dawson's saffron haddock soup, followed by roast peppered fillet of beef, rounded off by cranberry walnut tarts? Did it matter? It did matter – at least to Mary. It mattered to the point where the tension was racked-up to an unbearable degree for the whole of the preceding week, as preparations were made and innumerable shopping trips undertaken for what should have been a relaxing meal with friends.

Andrew laughed, and stuck Kingsley Amis back on the shelf. Life had its funny side. If you didn't laugh, you'd cry.

Even as he did so, however, Andrew's mind caught another thought – 'the need was past'. He'd read that somewhere, and it had made him feel uncomfortable at the time. The need for what had passed: the need to be civil to each other, the need to care for your love, and the need to be desired? Was the whole courting process simply a charade – a show without meaning?

Eliot's sad line – 'in the room the women come and go …' – came back to him, and he was reminded of chatter and dresses. The other great bane of dining out was that Mary never had anything to wear; this was also true all summer, during the barbecue season. A simple meal with friends meant piling debt on the credit card. Angrily, Andrew took down a snooker cue from the rack and played a game against an imaginary opponent.

He lost, and stepped out through the french windows onto the patio. It had taken him three months to dig that out, spadeful by spadeful, and cart the earth away. When it was completed, with the small fishpond in place, they had enjoyed many a spring or autumn meal, al fresco, sitting in the last rays of an evening sun. Andrew and his oldest boy would drink together there, enjoying a late whisky and cigar. It was there, too, that Amy had courted her first boyfriend and where Robert – as a child – had created his fantasy games. Sometimes they still found the little plastic figures buried in the earth of the flower borders.

Andrew called Madge, the spaniel, and walked out with her towards the park. He could hear Mary was still working in the lounge, and he didn't trouble to tell her that he was exercising the dog. Didn't he do so at about this time every evening? The park closed at dusk; he still had a short while.

He remembered how, as a young couple, they had laughed at the married people they met – married people weighed down by the trivia of marriage. They would never end up like that, would they? He and Mary had once listened to a married couple argue about a tablecloth – argued so vigorously that they had almost came to blows. It wasn't simply about the colour that the couple had disagreed, but also about the size, how it might come in for Christmas if they chose a certain style, where it was to be kept (and why the man insisted that it went into the dining room drawer), whether it would be easy to iron (and who did most of the ironing, anyway) and whether their friends would approve of their choice.

The argument simply rolled on, gathering energy from further grievances, until Andrew realised that the couple were not actually arguing about the tablecloth at all; the tablecloth was simply the catalyst. Andrew had understood it, seeing it in others, but could not apply the same perspicacity to his own problems.

Early on in their marriage, when Mary was looking after the three children, she often exploded at him when he arrived home from work. "It's all right for you. You get out to school every day. I'm stuck at home here with the children." He considered this unreasonable, since Mary had wanted both to have the children and be able to bring them up. After several of these corrosive encounters – behind closed doors after he had put the children to bed, between clenched teeth and hissed rather than spoken – he had lost his patience and said, simply "If you feel like that, you go out to work, and I'll stay at home and bring up the children. I'll enjoy that, and you'll be happy having to go to work every day. I'll resign for the end of the term". It had called her bluff, but solved nothing.

What seemed only days later, Mary had exploded again. Thinking back, as he stood overlooking the duck pond, Andrew could not quite recall what their next argument was about. He only knew it had occurred because he could remember his despair on thinking that he had closed down one vent, through which the volcano that was his wife could explode, only to have her find another further along the path.

He was not alone, and knew it. Listening to the humour at parties, Andrew was aware that most, if not all, marriages were the same. None of their friends had found marriage to be what they had expected. In one way or another they all seemed disenchanted, their lives bound together by a succession of disagreements over apparent trifles. Most hid behind humour, and some may have found their own means of escape – drink and adultery being, he suspected, on the cards for some of the men – but, for Andrew, each confrontation was a scouring of the soul. He sought harmony with a blind determination. He was not interested in escape and nor could he court such an idea.

He did not think of himself as foolish enough to expect marriage to be 'a bed of roses' (it was easier to use a phrase like that than to think through what it meant), and expected life with Mary (or any woman) to be discordant at times, but not regularly and not unless the reason was clear. Dissonance had become a habit and – like all habits – it was hard to break.

It wasn't even that they were unhappy most of the time; it was more that, when the discord did arise, it was acrimonious. It was the bitterness at those odd moments which he could not understand and, in the end, felt unable to tolerate.

Their children would not have been aware of this; they were not a couple who heaped their emotional outbursts onto the shoulders of their children. Such arguments as occurred happened out of their earshot. Life for the children was a good one – as it should have been, as it was a parent's duty to make it – and their family life was marked, as many of their friends had commented, by closeness. What, then, was the price he had paid for that concord?

He stopped off for a pint at The Woolpack on the way home. It was late November, and the cold had cut in early so the pub's log fire was roaring in the grate, and he settled down beside it. It was a rough pub in some ways, but it was comfortable. Madge enjoyed his visits because the landlord fussed her and the girl behind the bar always had a titbit ready. He felt content with the spaniel curled up under the table, and stayed for a second pint: it was Adnams Broadside and worth savouring.

He considered phoning Mary, asking her to join him, but decided against it. They would only end up talking about her imaginary problems – how could she meet her commitments to the church, the school, the family, the charities she supported, the WI, her evening class – all the way down the list to the man who ran the paper shop. What she could owe him Andrew failed to see, but there would be something – of that he had no doubt.

His decision not to phone made him feel mean, and so he thumbed in her number on his mobile. Her voice was weary, and she wondered where he had gone and why he hadn't told her he was going. She would have enjoyed the walk, but "no" she didn't want to turn out now: it was too late, and she was tired. If only he had asked her before, she might have come with him. How long would he be – they had to be up for work tomorrow, and she didn't want him rolling in drunk and waking her up.

Andrew couldn't remember ever having rolled in drunk, so why had she said that – was it spite, jealousy that he might be enjoying himself, concern that he was … doing something that didn't involve her?

His thoughts rolled on, and he cut them off, quickly – not, however, quickly enough to avoid a notion that had been ticking away in his mind all evening. It had first entered his surmises when Mary had dismissed Jodie Smith's motives as purely selfish. "She wanted him, and Elaine and the children were in the way". He didn't like the thought, although it was the central supposition of a story he sometimes told the children in his assemblies during his 'traditional tales' theme.

It cropped up in the Arthurian legends, and Chaucer had given it to the Wife of Bath. A knight or a king, in order to save the life of one or the other, rides out to seek an answer to the riddle 'What is the thing that women most desire?' On his journey, the usual answers flow from the ale houses and the markets – the places of tried and tested wisdom down the ages. "Wealth and riches", "to be honoured and important", "fine clothes and jewellery", "to be flattered and wooed", "jollity and pleasure", "fun in bed", "having no one to reprove us", "to be thought discreet, and not a gossip" were all offered in complete seriousness, but none satisfied the traveller as he sought wisdom. Eventually, on the last day of his quest, it is an old and ugly lady – 'a loathsome creature' – who gives him the answer. It is to "have their will", which Chaucer interprets as 'sovereignty over their husbands or lovers' and the original tale as simply 'getting their own way in all things'. In each case, the knight concedes to the will of the 'loathly lady' who then becomes beautiful, and they live happily ever after.

Andrew could think of women who would be out-raged by the story and others who might give, in private, a quiet and smiling nod to its truths. Either way, it wasn't something he could accept as the price of a happy marriage.

The house was quiet when Andrew arrived home. He wiped Madge and settled her down, gave her the regular bedtime chew, checked all the doors and windows, cleared any stray washing up, tidied the cushions, straightened the rugs, laid the table for breakfast and turned off all the lights.

Mary was asleep when he crept into the bedroom. She looked soft and gentle in a Victorian-style nightdress he had bought her from Past Times; it was a nightdress which held fond memories for him. He undressed quietly and got into bed beside her; it was warm, and Andrew cuddled, gently, into her back, curling his left arm around her and tucking his legs in under her thighs. Mary stirred but did not wake. She was a heavy sleeper, and there was no chance of her being roused.

In many respects, this kind of thing was what marriage was about – this being together, warm and safe, in a house that would take so many years of their lives in payment and as many more in turning it into a home. He felt untroubled as he dropped easily into sleep; tomorrow was another day, and he looked forward to his work.

Chapter 13

Sacrifice

"Did you know that Joy and Brian are having a conservatory built?" asked Mary, as they sat down for breakfast the next morning.

"No," replied Andrew, not wanting to know how this affected him.

"I wonder, sometimes, whether we would be better off with a conservatory."

"Where would we have one built?"

"Well, where the patio is. We could always re-build that further down the garden. It would be nice to walk out onto a patio from a conservatory. After all, if Joy and Brian can afford one I don't see why we can't. They can't cost that much."

Andrew thought of the back-breaking hours he had spent removing earth, barrow-load by barrow-load, and then in laying the concrete base to the patio before finally completing the tiling and pond, but said nothing. He didn't want an argument at the breakfast table.

He could feel Mary watching him, waiting for a response, and he muttered something he knew she would take as an agreement. It would keep her quiet. As it neared Christmas, there was so much on at school, and he couldn't face any distractions at the moment. His mind was on the Christingle, the early years' play, carols round the tree and the Father Christmas grotto, which he had yet to build. There were traditional parties to consider and his usual festive assemblies to work out in detail. A refusal to have a conservatory built over a cherished patio, which meant so much to him and had taken so many hours of his life to construct, could wait.

Christmas – their Christmas at home – was concentrated into two hectic weeks, but spread over a much wider and exhausting month. Their three children had returned from university far too early, Andrew thought. (Why didn't universities work the same length of term as other educational establishments?) There is always something extremely offensive – when working long, hard hours oneself – to come home to find other adults lounging around, wondering when dinner was going to be ready.

Left to himself, Andrew would probably have told them to "have it ready" when he and their mother got home from work – and, to be fair, they probably would have done so – but families don't work in that way. Mary didn't see how "the children", whose ages ranged from eighteen to twenty-two, could "possibly be expected to cater for themselves when they were at home". At the same time, of course, she was in no real position to cater for them, since she was as busy at work as Andrew. Somehow, Andrew always found himself caught in the middle of these situations.

When December 17th arrived – it had been a long autumn term – both he and Mary were shattered; the final explosion of parties had taken its toll. Although the quiet and atmospheric end-of-Christmas-term goodbye, involving carols around the tree with over three hundred children, had made Andrew realise why he loved the season, it had done nothing to remove the feeling of being absolutely exhausted. Andrew stuffed his briefcase under the well of his desk and collapsed into an easy chair by the fire, having poured himself a beer and Mary a grapefruit juice with a slimline tonic.

The children were all out somewhere – probably enjoying themselves with friends – and he was looking forward to a long and peaceful evening.

"You bought some beer, then, on the way home?"

"No. I didn't even think about it, I was that tired."

"Well, where did you get that one from? Jonathan said, this morning, that we were out of beer."

"It was one I hid in the flower pots on the patio."

"What?"

"It was one I ..."

"I heard what you said. I just couldn't believe it."

"I knew I'd feel like a beer when I got in tonight – it always seems to wind down the term nicely – and I knew that, unless I hid one, there would be none left. Either Jonathan or Robert or one of Amy's boyfriends would have drunk it."

"I can't believe that you'd be that selfish – to deny your own children a beer!"

"I'm not denying them anything. They've cleared both fridges since they've been home, and I didn't consider it particularly selfish to keep just one beer for myself."

"You could, at least, have bought some on the way home. They might bring friends round tonight."

"Well, in that case, perhaps they could bring some beer in with them. Give them a ring."

"You know they can't afford to buy beer – they're students!"

"Oh really? I imagine they buy enough when they're at university. They've all got the latest in mobile phones – which cost a packet – and have you seen Amy's wardrobe lately?"

"Well, if you begrudge your own children ..."

"I begrudge them nothing. I'm just sitting down – resting – after a long, hard term, and I'm drinking the one beer in the whole house which they haven't drunk. OK?"

"Well, don't get too comfortable. It's Christmas in three days, and there's a lot to do," stormed Mary, leaving the room and slamming the door.

She hadn't 'had her will' in the matter, but that gave Andrew no pleasure and he did not enjoy his pint.

Christmas was the long travail promised by Mary's slamming remark, and this thought disappointed Andrew. He always enjoyed Christmas at work, and had always enjoyed the festivities when the children were young, but this was no longer the case.

He had gone out for some beer; after all, he didn't want to be represented as mean to his children. As he left, Mary had called out, asking whether he could "just pick up a few Christmassy nibbles in case anyone came round". How he hated the word 'just'. He recalled so many occasions when he'd been heavily occupied by something that needed doing – pruning the shrubs, cleaning the car, vacuuming the lounge, laying the fire, cooking Sunday lunch – only to be asked, by 'the voice', whether he could "just" do something else. The request always implied that he wasn't doing anything or, if he was, it couldn't possibly be as important as whatever it was his wife was doing. Their run-up to Christmas had started on that disgruntled note.

December 22nd had been a leg-shattering round of cleaning and dusting and polishing and adding to the festive decorations, and, in-between times, making sure that "the children" were fed – breakfast, lunch and dinner.

This was followed, on the evening of the 22nd and the morning of the 23rd, by several rounds of shopping that almost beggared belief. Andrew knew that all the festive shopping, or ordering, had been completed on previous weekends. All meats (turkey, beef, pork and ham), Christmas speciality foods (cakes, dates, nuts, glace fruits, dried fruits and chocolates), Christmas speciality goods (crackers, napkins, party streamers and candles) and festive drinks (rum, port, brandy, sherry, soft drinks and mixers, which he'd hidden in the garden shed) had been seen to by himself or Mary. There could be nothing else to shop for – could there? It had been dealt with – hadn't it? No! How could anyone be expected to remember cling film, cake boards, greaseproof paper, cocktail sticks …? Mary's list went on and on, and she was obviously busy so could he "pop down" to the supermarket and get them, since he had to re-stock the beer, anyway?

This round of shopping was followed by the "essentials, which they didn't want to be without" (tea, coffee, bread, cream, eggs, cheese, fresh orange juice, salt and pepper …) and, finally, by the "last minute things" (potatoes, parsnips, carrots, Brussels sprouts, mushrooms, Bramley apples, oranges, grapes …).

While Andrew was rounding up the last of the shopping, Mary was busy in the kitchen, although he found himself actively engaged once he'd stumbled in with his multitude of bags. In this way, the 23rd merged with the 24th and a seemingly endless round of cooking. The vegetables were prepared, the trifle was made, the baking was done, the ingredients were weighed out for Christmas Day, the turkey was stuffed, various relishes made and the alarm clock set so that they "wouldn't be late getting the turkey in the oven".

There was no let-up on Christmas Day, either. They were up at 7 o'clock to pre-heat the oven and then began a remorseless, will-sapping journey through the cooking of the turkey, making sure "the children" had a good breakfast and, then, pre-lunch drinks, setting the table, warming the plates and serving dishes, un-wrapping the presents (such a delight when they really had been 'children'), cooking the devils-on-horseback, making the bread sauce, steaming the Christmas pudding, checking the turkey, parboiling and roasting the potatoes, roasting the parsnips, making the giblet gravy and boiling or steaming the sprouts, carrots and peas.

Had the journey ended, here, with the meal, which he enjoyed thoroughly, Andrew might have recovered – but it didn't end with the last mouthful of Christmas pudding. Andrew staggered from the table to face the mess in the kitchen. The washing-up was only part of it; much work was required, before he could reach the dishes, to wrap all the uneaten food in kitchen foil and find a place for it in the already bursting fridges.

Mary helped with this before disappearing to "tidy the lounge and put out some nuts and chocolates". No, she didn't think the children should have to help with the washing up – let them enjoy their Christmas. "You're only young once!" His eldest son's voice came through

from the lounge "Leave it, Dad – we'll see to it later".
He wouldn't, of course: it would still be there when
they came to serve supper. "It won't take a minute,"
Mary had said, and it was true – it didn't take her a
minute because Andrew did most of it himself. Robert
and Amy wandered through, sleepy with food and
drink, when he had more or less finished, and Mary
told him that "she knew the children would help,
and was he going to get a game started now and get
everybody a drink?"

At that point, Andrew felt pleased that he had
already wiped dry the carving knife and replaced it in
the cutlery drawer. He was, when all was said and
done, a civilized man and didn't like to ask "When do
I get a rest?"

He sat brooding over Christmas, while checking
the cost on his credit card, and he wondered. It was the
New Year, the children had returned to university and –
being back at work – he was happy again. He had settled
into the routines that kept him sane. At the same time, he
was aware of a certain remorselessness which seemed
to drive them on – but to where, and for what purpose?
He was aware, also, that he resented the pressure.

Asked about it, afterwards, everyone would say that
they had enjoyed Christmas, that there was nothing like
a get-together, that Christmas was a family time ... and
all the usual clichés, and yet it wasn't true, or – at least
– not completely true. The only ones who really enjoyed
Christmas were the young – those from whom no effort
was required. For the adults, it was a hard slog at an
enormous cost. He knew his card would not be clear
until after Easter at the earliest. There was nothing left
about Christmas that had anything to do with its

meaning; it had become a treadmill that everyone felt obliged to work – a wearisome and monotonous routine, and he saw no ending.

It was unfortunate that Mary chose that moment to come into the study and wonder if they were going on holiday that year. She emphasised the 'if' as though they never went on holiday, or as though it always took a tremendous effort on her part to persuade Andrew to do so. In fact, there wasn't one year he could recall when they hadn't gone somewhere, whether they could afford it or not, and then spent until Christmas (or beyond) paying off the card. It was unfortunate, too, that she added "after all, everyone else is booking up now and if we don't do so soon we might not get what we want".

Andrew nodded at the credit card bill and pushed it across the table towards her, but – again, unfortunately – Mary shrugged it off.

"It's just something that has to be paid," she said, "Other people have the same expenses, and they seem to cope."

"I'm not other people, and I resent the suggestion that I cannot cope. I manage quite well to run a large primary school – and its budget has never been in the red. Tell you what – I'll transfer this lot to your credit card, and you can take out a festive loan to pay it. Let me know when you have, and then we'll start thinking about a summer holiday."

He had rarely spoken to her like that before, and Mary was, for the moment, flabbergasted. The moment passed quickly, however, and she struck back.

"When I think of the sacrifices I make for the family ..."

"Like what? We hear a lot these days about the sacrifices women make. Let's hear one."

"You get more and more like your father every day. You're ruthless, Andrew, and there's no good you denying it, but if you think you can bully me – if you think I'm going to play the 'little woman', you've got another think coming."

Mary, when roused, often compared him to his father (with whom he had never got on), and considered this the highest insult. In a moment, she would insult his mother – he knew that, and waited.

"Your mother has been content, all her life, to sit at home and go nowhere, but I'm not like that. I need a holiday. I can't go on working the way I do, if there isn't a holiday to look forward to."

"You don't have to work. We can live on my salary. You work because you choose to do so."

"Live on your salary?"

"Yes. Of course, we wouldn't be kitting Amy out for the London Fashion Week every time she goes to the cinema, and we wouldn't be spending a couple of thousand pounds on Christmas – but do we need to?"

"Most normal men ..."

"I'm not 'most men', although I do consider myself fairly 'normal' – I'm me, whatever that is ... perhaps I should find out. What's that mantra the feminist brigade is always chanting – 'If you don't like your life, change it'? Perhaps I will. If you'd be kind enough to give me a divorce, I'll make a fresh start."

Mary glared at him. He had never seen such hate in her eyes before – or was it hate? No – it was fear. He'd never been appreciated because he'd always been there. The problem for Mary's generation of women was that they had nothing genuine of which to complain. Ever since the 70s, his generation of men had simply got stuck in and done as much around the house and for the children as had their wives. There wasn't one man he could think of in his circle of friends who wasn't as capable of running a home as their wives – and, indeed, did. Nothing to complain about and yet the moaning never stopped. If it wasn't Christmas, it was next year's holiday. If it wasn't about how hard it was being a 'working mother' (as though there wasn't such a thing as a 'working father'), it was about how difficult it was at work.

"There's another woman, isn't there?" screamed Mary.

"No."

"Oh, don't be ridiculous – of course there is. It's not the young girl – the one who took Julian Price away from his wife? … It's not Elaine Price! You've been having a lot to do with her, haven't you? … You need to get yourself sorted out, Andrew. Christmas was bad enough with you and your moods. I'm not having this going on all year, right through to the summer."

Mary slammed out of the room, and Andrew sighed with relief. He walked to the french windows and looked out at the dark, winter's night. Out there, somewhere was freedom. Freedom from …? He knew what he felt, but his feelings were only safe as thoughts, at the moment. It would take some while before he dared to put them into words.

Book Two

CHAPTER 14

Mary and the children

It was now three months since Andrew Mansell had asked Mary for a divorce. Obviously, she had not taken him seriously. What wife, after nearly a quarter of a century of marriage, would? Their life had gone on much as before – the usual round of winter parties, dinner dates, visits to the theatre, weekend rambles and planning for the future. They had even organised their summer holiday, which was designed to "invigorate their marriage". Once it was established that none of the children wanted to go away with them, Mary had suggested that they take a cruising holiday in France – a country they both loved in the way their kind of Brit loved France: the culture, the food, the ambience, the pace of life, the weather ... This was to be shared with Mary's sister and her husband, and promised to be fun.

It was at the end of April, when his two younger children had returned to university, that Andrew went to see the solicitor for the first time. He was surprised when she mentioned an organisation called Relate; she explained that she was obliged to do so. He had never heard of this counselling service and indicated that it would not be appropriate. He noticed that she held his eyes for just a fraction of a second when he said, in answer to her question, that nobody else was involved. She explained that if adultery was not the reason for the divorce then he would have to put forward grounds that would show the "irretrievable breakdown" of the marriage. Andrew agreed to return in a week's time with a list of reasons.

He was pleased with the week's respite because he needed to see his children, individually, and this would involve a long journey – first to Newcastle to see his second son, Robert, and then down to Essex to see his daughter, Amy. Jonathan, still lounging around at home and wondering how best to use his gap year, would have to wait until last. He had told Mary he was on a weekend course at Belstead House, where the LEA held teachers' courses, knowing this was the only way he could fit in such a marathon drive.

Robert received his declaration in 'stunned silence'; the phrase came into Andrew's mind as he watched the boy's face, and he felt sorry for his son. He would, he thought, have 'done anything to spare him this', but then accepted that he was actually sitting at the kitchen table in his son's digs talking about divorcing the boy's mother.

Robert turned his back on his father, walked over to the kettle and offered him another cup of coffee. Andrew didn't want one, but accepted. He didn't know what else to do – going out for a meal seemed out of order, somehow.

"What's Mum going to do?"

"I haven't told her, yet, about going to the solicitor. I wanted to see you, Amy and Jonathan first. So don't contact her until after the weekend, please. Give me a chance to speak to her."

"There's no one else, you say?"

"No."

"In that case, I don't understand why you are doing this."

"It's between Mum and me. I can't talk about it – it wouldn't be right."

"No, I can see that."

Robert didn't sit down at the table, but walked across the room and stood looking at the wall.

"What's going to happen to the home?"

Andrew was surprised at the question, especially since he considered his second son to be unselfish. He thought, perhaps, he had expected some enquiry as to how he felt about what he was proposing. Looking at his son's back, he remembered that this was the child who had thanked them for his upbringing. This was the quiet one who spent so much time in his room playing games on his computer; the room was buried deep within the house, and was his son's refuge and study. It was from here that he would saunter into the lounge and join the family on a winter's night, bringing with him a board game round which they would all gather.

It was significant that he had recalled a winter's night. They played games all year round but it was a winter's night that he remembered best, when the cold was shut out and all was warm and snug. Andrew reassured Robert that the house would remain the family home. After that, they said little more to each other but shook hands, as they had always done, and patted each other on the back.

"I suppose you know what you're doing, Dad," said Robert, as he shut the front door behind his father.

Andrew drew up outside the residential tower blocks of Essex University, and thought how much he preferred the ivy walls of Newcastle. When they brought Amy down for the first time, he'd noticed that the windows could only be opened a certain distance, and had been told that this was to prevent students jumping if the exam pressure became too great or they had failed. He hadn't been sure whether or not the third year student who told him this had been joking.

Amy listened quietly, with the same intensity as her brother, and then exploded.

"It's the male menopause, Dad – that's all it is! You're not going to break up the family because of that, are you?"

"The male menopause is a nonsensical concept. It's just something to give the summer newspapers and the glossy magazines something to write about."

"I don't get my ideas from glossy magazines."

"Then perhaps it's just the current wisdom of the campus to which I'm being subjected. Whatever – it has nothing to do with my feelings or my thoughts. I've not gone into this lightly, Amy, and I'm not breaking up the family."

"Oh, come on, Dad – get real. How did Mum take it? What did she have to say?"

Andrew repeated what he had told Robert, insisting that Amy stayed off her mobile until he'd had a chance to talk to Jonathan. He saw her hesitate as he spoke, and took it that she credited him with serious intentions.

"Perhaps the term 'menopause', as related to men, is silly since what men go through at that age doesn't compare with what women have to endure, but it's not nonsense, Dad. You're dissatisfied with your life – more than half-way through and wonder what you've achieved, your marriage seems stale to what it once promised, you're low on the list of Mum's priorities, you're hemmed in by her social dos and don'ts, you've had her losing her temper with you once a month every month for over twenty years or whenever she can't get her own way over something, you sit there every evening listening to a breakdown of how difficult her day at work has been, you've got three children who – apparently – don't need you anymore ... Am I getting close?"

Andrew looked at his daughter and laughed. How the hell was she so clever, and yet so young? Perhaps there was hope for the next generation? Perhaps they would cut their way through the crap? He hoped so.

"It isn't going to change, Amy. You're right – up to a point. I'm in my late forties and might live another forty or fifty years, and none of what you have just said is going to change."

"How do you know? You haven't talked to Mum."

"Amy?" he said with a quizzical look that made her laugh.

"All right – she'll hit the roof as soon as you open your mouth and then rush off to bake cakes for the WI. But that's life, Dad."

"Is it? Think over what you're saying and its implications for me for the next half of my life – and I repeat, 'is it'?

It was his daughter's turn to feel a chill pass through her, and Andrew saw it in the sudden pallidness of her complexion and the flash of anger from her eyes.

"It won't be any different with another woman."

"Won't it?"

"Is there another woman?"

"No."

"Truth?"

"Truth."

She came over to where Andrew was sitting on the rather hard plastic settee and put her arms round him as only his daughter did. Robert felt the same for him – Andrew knew that – but his affection was unspoken and passed across by look rather than touch. They sat for a long while without speaking, and then Amy suggested that they went for a meal. It didn't have to be a student pub, she said, and her boyfriend didn't have to come with them, she replied, when Andrew asked the question.

During the meal, at The Hole in the Wall, which they both enjoyed, neither spoke specifically of Andrew's intentions but Amy talked endlessly about happiness. Happiness, she said, was in loving another to the exclusion of all else – thinking their thoughts, feeling their feelings, knowing their desires. It was only through giving yourself to another person in that way and in knowing them so deeply that true happiness and, therefore, true freedom could be found. He wondered at first what she had been reading, but then realized he had thought like that at her age. He wondered at the sincerity of it all, and saw no link between such beliefs and the reality of everyday life. Could one transcend reality? How?

"You will reconsider, won't you, Dad?" Amy said as they parted.

He smiled but promised nothing, realising that he was past the point where he wished to hold out false hopes to anyone, least of all his children who – despite appearances – he loved.

He used his daughter's room that night and returned home early on the Sunday afternoon to maintain the impression that he had been on a weekend course. Mary and Jonathan had just finished a late lunch, and Andrew asked his son if he'd like to go for a drink. He knew Mary wouldn't come, since she always settled down to prepare her next week's lessons on Sunday afternoons.

Andrew took Madge, the spaniel, and they walked her first in Christchurch Park. It was there, sitting in the Arboretum, that Andrew explained his intentions for the third time in two days. Jonathan's reaction was forthright and unequivocal.

"You're going to ruin everything. What is it you want out of life, Dad?"

Andrew looked at his son and thought 'freedom', but said nothing because that would have involved saying too much. He would have had to explain what he meant by the word.

"You and Mum don't argue. We've always said – Amy and Jonathan and me – that we've never heard you argue. We're known as a 'close' family – everyone says so. You've no money worries – well, no more than anyone else with three children of university age. Anyway, separating from Mum will only make that worse – not better. We all get on together. You're easy-going with us. There're no problems. We've got a nice home – tidy but comfortable. You can lounge around without feeling you have to plump up the cushions when you leave the room. We can bring our friends round. We talk about things. You know – religion, politics, literature, and so on. We've always felt free to express an opinion … This is going to ruin everything."

Jonathan paused and looked at his father, as though expecting him to agree that life was good and that he had everything for which to be thankful. Andrew felt that his silence was resented, but didn't see how he could say anything without betraying that knowledge which existed only between him and Mary. He remembered his own father opening his heart to him once, and how he resented being told things about his mother – things he didn't want to know, things he felt he ought not to know.

"I thought you'd be looking forward to the years ahead. We'll soon be off your hands, going our own way in the world. I'd have thought you and Mum had everything to look forward to."

"You can't escape the past – what has been affects the present. Those differences that lie between us are not going to go away. People get into habits which become a lifestyle – unbreakable. What 'is', remains forever. People do not change – not once the lifestyle has been set."

"You and Mum went straight into marriage, didn't you? You never thought about it, did you? You just 'fell in love', and got married. My generation is going to be more careful. We're going to get to know each other first, and our marriages will be stronger for it."

"Let's hope that turns out to be true."

"Can we go, now? It's cold out here."

Jonathan stopped off at The Woolpack for a drink, saying he'd give his father time to talk to his mother, "if he still felt he had to". There was an almost desperate hope in the young man's voice as he urged his father to think carefully about what he was doing.

"You've done what?" screamed Mary, "How dare you lie to me and go round talking to your children. I'll put them straight about you."

"I wanted to see them first …"

"So they would see it your way, no doubt."

"No. I just wanted to tell them what I intended to do. I didn't go into the reasons why."

"Well, that's very thoughtful of you, Andrew. Perhaps you'd care to tell me?"

"No, I wouldn't. It's quite obvious that if I so much as open my mouth the screaming will go on all night. If you run your mind back over everything which has caused a disagreement between us over the last twenty years or so, you'll be able to work it out for yourself."

"My God, you don't half harbour grudges."

"Each time we've had a disagreement – however trivial – over the last twenty years, every grievance you've ever had against me has come pouring out, and I've had to sit there soaking it up. Cast your mind back over those grievances – real or imagined – and you'll have some idea of why I asked you for a divorce last Christmas. I've never come up to scratch for you, have I Mary? Well, now, you've got the chance to find someone who will."

"God, you're ruthless."

"There – you see – you've got two good reasons to be grateful. I harbour grudges and I'm ruthless."

"All women say things like that to their husbands."

"Do they? Well, perhaps they shouldn't. Perhaps men don't actually like it. Moreover, perhaps they shouldn't have to put up with it."

As soon as he had returned without Jonathan, Mary knew something was in the air. The tension – normally, so absent in the home – had resonated. Mary had been in the kitchen, preparing herself a supper drink, and Andrew had entered through the french windows, leaving Madge in the study, which was unusual. He had come straight to the point, knowing that discussion would be impossible. All he wanted to do now was to get away from the sound of her voice.

"Do you realise how humiliating this will be for me?" she said, "You could have left it until the end of the summer term. How do you think I'm going to concentrate on my job now?"

He didn't answer: what she said was true, but he had feared that postponing the decision would result in it never being made. The whole of the spring term, Andrew had steeled himself for that visit to the solicitor. He hadn't been sure when the decisive moment came but it had seemed to be when he was forced into complying with the holiday wishes. Somehow, he couldn't face the long build up – the endless planning towards something that wasn't going to happen.

He had worried about the children. Amy had first year exams to face, but he felt her intelligence would carry the day, and he knew Robert would switch off and focus his mind. He could have stuck it out for another three or four years until his daughter had completed her course, but Andrew couldn't face more time in the marriage. Yes, it had been a selfish decision; he couldn't hide from the fact.

"Stay until the end of the term, at least," said Mary, very calmly, "Give the children a chance to complete their exams, and give us a chance to do what we said we'd do over the summer – the barbecues, the holiday, the weekends away with our friends – you know ... you owe me that, Andrew."

How much can turn on a phrase? Always, in their arguments, she reminded him of what he owed her, of how much she had sacrificed for him, of what she had given up – but he never saw it as she did. It didn't seem to Andrew that Mary had given up a great deal; it seemed to him that she had got what she wanted – a husband, a home and a family. Yet, always, there was this dissatisfaction – as though he had failed her, failed to deliver what he had promised when they were married. He failed to see what more he could have done, and was tired – so very tired – of making the effort. He felt relieved as he looked at her, knowing that not only he – but Mary, also – was free. She could find the man he had never been and start a new life.

He listened as she spoke – as the anger turned to pleading – but he had heard it all before, so many times. He knew that before long, if she did not get her way, the anger would return, but it didn't bother him. 'You owe me that, Andrew.' First, you find that you owe your parents, and then your wife, and then your children, and then – forever after – your wife. Does it go on like that for all eternity? Do you never get to the point when all you owe has been paid, your duty done – and you can turn to thinking about yourself?

"You think you can just walk out of here, turn your back on us – your family – and start a new life as though we had never existed."

"That's an awful thing to say, and it isn't true," replied Andrew, keeping his voice calm.

"Hhmm! You sound like your father. His voice always went very quiet and reasonable after he'd insulted you."

"I haven't insulted …"

"Haven't insulted me! What do you call this?"

There was no answer he could give. Already, he could see that Mary's mind was absorbing the social fall-out.

How would she explain to her friends? How would her sister react? Would Elspeth be quietly pleased? There had always been jealousy between them; would the older sister be the one whose marriage had worked, while Mary's had failed?

"Who will I have to talk to, now? You haven't considered me in all this. All you thought about is what you want ... There isn't another woman, is there?"

He had wondered when she would ask that question, and was surprised that it had taken so long.

"No."

"It might be easier if there was – at least people would understand that. Now, they'll blame me."

His heart was breaking as she spoke. He did not know how he could listen to the woman he loved – the mother of his children – and do nothing to comfort her. He also knew that once he put his arms round her shoulders, once he tried to calm her and talk her down, it would all be over. Life would settle down again, the old routines would take over, and he'd wait for the next outburst of discontentment.

Andrew was determined to hold on. So many times before, after hours of lacerating verbal abuse, he had come to this point, and pulled back. As he stood watching her, deliberately immobile, making no move to bring the comfort he had always brought, Mary released him from his sense of obligation. It was only for a moment, but a moment is sometimes enough.

"You're like your mother, aren't you?" she snapped, "Stoical."

She thought it one of the greatest insults she could hurl, and she had done so many times. For Andrew to be stoical like his mother, for him not to rise in anger against the onslaught of her words – was anathema to Mary.

"I don't think we're going to get much further, tonight, are we?" he said, aware that his very choice of words contained a dishonesty of intent. He wasn't concerned that their conversation should get any further. He just wanted to get away, but he knew that the words implied a hope to Mary, and that this might quieten her – at least for the moment. "Jonathan will be back in a moment. We'd best get to bed."

"You'll be here in the morning?" she asked.

"Yes. I'll sleep on the settee in the study tonight."

As Andrew turned from her, Mary didn't try to stop him as he had expected, and he reached the study door without being molested. He knew that, once inside, he could lock the door against her; he couldn't bear the thought of her pursuing him tonight. How many times before, as he retreated from a row, had she hounded him round the garden?

"If you do this, you'll never spend another Christmas with your children."

"How can you know that?"

"Because I shall see that you don't," she replied in a voice that sent a chill through his heart.

CHAPTER 15

The wisdom of Jack Tate

It was a fortnight later that Jack Tate strode purposefully into Andrew's office before school started in the morning. This was unusual because Jack normally arrived for work just before the caretaker closed the gates to avoid any likelihood of the parents' cars running over any children who might be dropped off in the car park.

"I'm not sticking my nose into your business, Andrew. I don't want to know about the gossip going round. I just want to know whether it's true that you and Mary are getting a divorce."

Andrew had left his home during the previous week. He had left quietly by the simple expedient of arriving home early one evening, packing his belongings into his car and driving away. Andrew had known that Mary would not be home at that time, and, fortunately, Jonathan had been out visiting a friend. Andrew had rented a small cottage at Chelmondiston and for the past ten days had driven 'home' across the Orwell Bridge. He had nicknamed it 'Freedom Bridge' because each night as he crossed the river a huge weight seemed to fall from his shoulders.

"Yes," he replied, without showing any interest in where Jack had got his information or exhibiting any surprise that the gossip had moved so quickly, "it's true."

"Then we'd better have a talk, son, before this goes too far. Fancy a drink, tonight?"

"Will The Golf be OK?"

Settled with Andrew and a couple of pints of Fullers' London Pride by a lone window that looked out over the children's play area, Jack Tate wandered around before getting to the point.

"The only reason I'm sticking my nose into your business, Andrew, is because I like you. We all like you – you're a good head. You support your staff and the school's come on by leaps and bounds since you took over ... I don't want to see you do something you'll live to regret, that's all."

"I understand that, Jack – and thanks for the compliments."

"They're true – everyone says so. Your door's always open, and you never clobber us with all the government bullshit pouring out of Whitehall. Your first thought is for us and the children, and we appreciate that – Foxhall Primary is a nice place to work. You keep the pressure off, and everyone benefits – the staff, the children, the parents ..."

"But?"

"There're no 'buts'. I'm just saying this so that you'll know why I'm sticking my nose into your private life. It's purely selfish – I don't want to see you go under."

"You think I'm under pressure at work?"

"I think that's part of it – and your age. You're late forties, aren't you?"

Jack Tate must have caught an expression verging on weariness passing across Andrew's face; perhaps it was something that flickered behind his eyes, Andrew thought, because he was sure that he had kept smiling.

"I've been through it, son. I know."

Jack was past sixty and edging towards retirement. He was the kind of teacher referred to as "one of the old school": not the easiest type to carry forward, but actually kind to the children and with a genuine ability to teach. He paused again and looked at Andrew, seemingly aware that the younger man was tired and not wanting to listen.

"What you're doing, Andrew, is going to cause you and your family more pain than you can imagine. I don't think you'll lose the respect of the staff because they like you, but you'll lose your self-respect and – if you're not careful – that'll bring you down."

He poured the remainder of the first pint down his throat and nodded at Andrew, who shook his head. When Jack came back from the bar, his second pint in his hand, he seemed to have made up his mind to carry on with what he might have felt sounded like a sermon.

"Women are all the same. Once you know one, you know them all. They've all got their eye on the main chance. When you get married, in your twenties, it's all eagerness, isn't it? That can't wait for it, and they can't get enough of it – and then it goes flat. They've fulfilled themselves, see – they've fulfilled their need to have children and you've served your purpose. It's called the 'biological imperative'. Basically, women aren't interested in sex – except as a means of getting their man. We enjoy it, but they just use it. It's a tool – it secures them what they want. Ever wondered why wives find it easier to forgive an affair than their husbands do? It's because, as I say, sex isn't that important to them – not to most of them, anyway … but we go on hungering for it, don't we, and it leads us into all sorts of trouble – especially at your age."

Andrew, at this stage in the 'conversation' was unsure of Jack Tate's drift. He wondered, for a time, whether the older men was about to advocate a course of serial adultery or eager to urge Andrew to a better understanding of his wife's nature. He had some sympathy for the sentiment 'once you know one, you now them all', although he would have added the word 'well' after the 'one'. Certainly, he found he had understood women better since his marriage. He was sure, however, that the rest of Jack's assertions would have met with vigorous denials in female company.

"You're at an age when you realise – consciously or not – that life doesn't go on for ever, and you're wondering what you've missed. Everyone depends on you – wife, family, colleagues. Am I right? How many nights do you arrive home without finding your wife wants to go on and on about 'her day', or the kids need taking somewhere? How many mornings do you arrive at work and there isn't some colleague's problem to sort out? And there's no release, is there – nothing to take your mind off things, nothing to make you think life's worth living? You look back and realise the dreams you had as a young man have faded, but the desire is still there. You think that out there, somewhere, is someone – a woman, of course – who is like-minded, and she is a shoulder to sigh on. Men need romance – women don't. Who writes the most romantic poetry or love songs – men! Most women, by the time they reach your age, have built their nest – it's just a question of making it a bigger and better nest."

Jack paused, dramatically. Andrew doubted that he had ever made this speech to anyone before, but was in no doubt that he had rehearsed it many times. Jack nodded at Andrew's half-drunk pint and indicated the bar. Andrew frowned, took Jack's glass and returned with two pints; he felt he had to keep the other man company.

"Besides, your 'biological imperative' is different to theirs – you need to 'put it about', as the saying goes. Women know this – they know it when they're young, and they know it even more certainly when they reach your age. It's easy to lure a man of your age, Andrew – you're vulnerable – and if the older woman's cock bird has flown the nest, there's a younger little hen waiting to furnish him with one."

It suddenly dawned on Andrew that Jack Tate assumed he had another woman, and he wondered who the staff gossips supposed this to be. It also occurred to him that Jack had been through a similar experience when he had been Andrew's age. Despite what the older man was saying, however, there was no bitterness in his tone: just a matter-of-fact acceptance of life through his eyes. Andrew was annoyed by Jack's assumptions and by many of the things he was saying, but was curious enough to want to hear the older man out. His words talked of the romantic nature of a man's vision, but they implied an attitude that was quite the reverse.

"Am I at least striking a chord on some points?" asked Jack, with more humility than his words suggested.

"Yes – go on, but do you think we ought to order some food with this drink?"

"You can, but my wife will have dinner ready when I get back – if you don't mind," replied Jack, "I can see why you're doing what you're doing, Andrew, but there's no need to destroy your marriage in the process."

He paused, clearly reluctant to continue, looked at Andrew with watery eyes, and then said "Yes, I went through a similar experience – most red-blooded men do – but I didn't let it ruin my marriage or break up my family."

"Did you love the other woman?"

"I thought I did, at the time," replied Jack, his eyes hard and knowing.

"Your wife found out?"

"Yes."

"But you got together again?"

"Yes … but it's best if they don't find out. It's never easy afterwards."

"I appreciate your honesty, Jack. This can't have been easy for you."

"It's a relief to talk about it – in some ways … It'll burn itself out, Andrew, in a year, at the most. Affairs don't last. You're being used, so don't have any compunction about ending it … Women are more down-to-earth than men. We make an enormous thing of sex. It means a lot to us – it's … a liberating experience. Women are more realistic … End it – get back to your family – secure your home."

Andrew didn't like to tell Jack that there was no other woman; he felt that his colleague might feel foolish. At the same time, he realised that he was continuing a deceit if he allowed the lie to linger.

"I'm not sure that my situation is quite like yours was, Jack", he muttered.

"We all imagine that our particular affair is unique, Andrew – after all, sex is unique, isn't it? I mean unique each time with each woman – no two are the same – not in bed."

"Who are the gossips linking me with? You see – there isn't another woman."

"Andrew, I'm not interested in who she is, or in what the women at work are saying," said Jack, the expression in his eyes suggesting that he was offended. "Just don't deceive yourself. I'm only trying to save you a great deal of pain, that's all. I shan't mention it again – unless you want a shoulder to cry on," he laughed. "Men don't go in for that sort of thing, do they? ... Look, I must go. As I say, my wife will have the dinner on, and she hates me being late."

Andrew watched the other man lurch slightly as he stood and then make his way to the swing doors. He turned and smiled as he left. Andrew looked at the menu: sausage, egg and chips – they served it all day. It sounded all right, and would give him time to burn off the alcohol before going home – or, at least, where he now lived.

CHAPTER 16

The enchantment of freedom

As he drove back across the Orwell Bridge that evening, Andrew realized he was not fully happy. He had achieved a kind of freedom, but it was one that hung heavily both on his conscience and his time. Prior to his move, he had been perceived as a nice, ordinary man who was good at his work and looked after his family. Now, he had joined the ranks of the … of the what – the separated, the divorced, the detached, the … degenerate?

He felt fragmented, and he knew that he was losing (or had already lost) his sense of humour. Previously, his conversation with Jack Tate would have tapped into his love of the ridiculous, and he would have enjoyed caricaturing the man's views: now, he took them seriously.

He was preparing to sever his links with a woman who he had known for the best part of a quarter of a century. He was preparing to split his family. The term 'broken home' was no longer used, and this was – perhaps – because it was too near the truth. 'Dysfunctional' suggested something that could be made to work – given the right treatment; 'broken' suggested something that – even if repaired – would never be quite the same again. Try as you might to disregard the cracks, they would still be visible to all.

'Close' had often been used to describe his family, and it was true. The rows he heard about in other homes never occurred in their house. Thinking back, it seemed to him that it had been both his and Mary's love for the children which had been the binding factor – not their regard for each other. 'Not in front of the children' may have been reduced to an almost comic phrase in the popular imagination, but it had been their guiding light. Disputes had been confined to those hours when the children were out or, when younger, asleep. They had taken place behind firmly-shut doors.

The lack of happiness in Mary had been one of the reasons for his decision to divorce her. It seemed to him that if he had been unable to make her happy during their twenty-odd years of marriage he was unlikely to do so over the next twenty. He remembered his sister-in-law laughing uproariously – during one of their Friday evening get-togethers with a couple of bottles of wine and some bread and cheese – when he had advanced the idea that bringing each other happiness was, surely, one of the purposes of being married. Elspeth had obviously dismissed the idea as an unworkable nonsense, and this saddened Andrew. It also produced, later in the evening when they had returned home, one of those long, bonding conversations between him and Mary, in which they exulted in agreeing with one another. They had made love afterwards, and Andrew had lain awake for a long time when his wife dropped off to sleep, completely at peace with himself.

Mary had once explained her outbursts (on one of those rare occasions when she acknowledged her monthly verbal abuse of him) by saying she only behaved that way because she wanted everything to be perfect, and became fearful when there was friction. In the early days of their married life, Andrew had traced his wife's fears back to her own home life: she had told him of the rows. As the years moved on, however, it seemed to him that this – as either reason or excuse – no longer held water: if they were happy, why the ill-temper?

Looking back, now, he could not help but wonder whether his in-laws expectations of married life were not more realistic, and whether – in concealing their own differences – he and Mary had done their own children a disservice.

On the other hand, he had no doubts in his own mind that he could not have tolerated his children being brought up in a home where rows, disputes, disagreements, arguments – call them what you will – were accepted as natural. This firm belief had been one of the reasons why – soon after his first child, Jonathan, had started school – Andrew had taken over the cooking of the breakfasts. Mary, who at that time was obviously not working as a teacher, would get up – irritated and snappy – "with everything to do". 'Everything' meant getting the children dressed, Jonathan off to school and cooking the breakfasts. Rather than have his children brought up in what he privately described as a 'bear garden', Andrew took over the breakfasts. He did this but saw no reason for the necessity. Mary was, after all, a full-time housewife – a role he quite happily offered to take on himself, if she preferred to go out to work.

This had been about seven years into their marriage, and Andrew reflected that it must have been here when the relationship began to disintegrate – when the rot began to set in. He had been expected not only to hold down a job, but to continue to play a major part in running the home. Why?

He had always 'done his fair share with the children' – the cleaning, the feeding, the nappy-changing, the bedtime rituals ... and all – but saw no reason why he should continue to run the house. Mary had been at home for five years at that time – from the birth of their first child – and wasn't that part of the marriage down to her?

He had said nothing, of course; he couldn't see the point of causing a row. Perhaps that had been his first mistake? Perhaps, if he had pointed out to Mary that he had a career to run, while she had the house, the resentment might have been avoided. Perhaps – but Andrew didn't think so. Experience had, albeit later, taught him otherwise: the more you did, the more you could.

These thoughts troubled his mind as he drew into the driveway of his rented country cottage. Troubled? They disordered him – a man who loved and needed order. His mind was in a state of anarchy, and he trembled as he pulled on the brake. He heard Madge barking a greeting as he scrambled out of the car. She was ready for her evening walk – something they always enjoyed together as soon as he arrived at the cottage. One or two steps to the front door and she would be leaping and yapping about his legs, but Andrew couldn't reach the door. He made for the side gate that led into the garden, rocking back and forth. It was quiet in the back garden, and it was secluded. There was a spot at the far end, beneath an apple tree where he could fall and rest.

Once there, Andrew collapsed, hugging himself against the tree. He couldn't move – at least not as he wanted to move; he was unable to stand. A cold sweat poured over him as he lay rolling on the ground. He was frightened, and the fear made him want to vomit, but all he could do was wretch until the muscles of his face ached. His arms clasped him tightly around the chest, but otherwise he could not move. His legs refused to do anything but tuck themselves up under his abdomen. His head would turn neither right nor left, but only nuzzle the ground. He began to shake and to sway backwards and forwards. Cries of anguish reached his mouth and he seemed to croak into the air. He didn't want anyone to find him like this, but he did want someone to pick him up, cuddle him and tell him that it would be all right.

How long this lasted, he was unsure, but it appeared to be only a short time. He became aware that Madge, who must have come out through the backdoor dog flap, was licking his face and looking distressed as she watched him. He felt sorry for her and managed to sit up.

"It'll be all right," he said, quietly, while still unable to reach out and reassure her, "we'll go for a walk soon, but first I must have a cup of tea – very sweet tea. Don't ask me why it must be sweet, Lady – I know I don't normally take sugar."

After a time, he rolled to his knees and, eventually, to his feet. They made their way into the kitchen where they sat together – she with a biscuit and he with a quiet cup of tea.

It was early the following week, after a lonely but peaceful weekend (during which he had not answered the phone despite having given the number to his children) that Andrew met Elaine Price – once again, at one of their interminable cluster meetings after school finished for the day.

"I'd much rather be preparing my lessons for tomorrow," she said.

"Me, too," replied Andrew.

"You still teach – with a school as large as Foxhall Primary?"

"It's one of the things that keep me sane. I can't imagine just going to work and sitting in my office all day processing yet more paperwork. What are we in education for if not to teach children?"

"Not all heads see it like you. Ours is a very nice chap, but some weeks he's hardly in school at all, and when he's there he's stuck in his office."

"Well, we all do things differently," replied Andrew, not wishing to be drawn on how another headteacher approached their work.

He felt Elaine must have understood his reluctance because she smiled and then looked down at her feet. When she spoke, however, Andrew realised that her head's work pattern was the last thing on her mind.

"I'm sorry to hear about you and Mary," she said.

"I'd no idea the news had travelled across the town so quickly."

"It's getting on for three weeks, Andrew. Some of your staff have been out to Chelmondiston to see where you're living."

The news shocked him. Had he been given to extravagant thoughts, Andrew would have said he felt 'violated'; as it was, he simply resented the invasion of his privacy.

"Teaching is a small world. I found that out when Julian left. There were people who knew before I did – and knew more than I did."

"Gossips know very little – they just think they do."

"That may be the case, but gossip becomes the accepted truth. You've left Mary. Who's the other woman? I expect they were hoping to find a car they knew in your driveway."

"How do you know the cottage has a driveway?"

"Andrew – we even know what's in the hanging baskets."

Andrew didn't laugh, and it wasn't a good feeling. There was a time when he would have found that snippet of information funny. Elaine smiled at him, looking him in the eyes this time.

"You just wanted to escape, didn't you? Just get away and be quiet?"

"Yes."

"I can tell you that your staff all support you. You're well thought of."

"Thank you. People have been kind ... and some have been ... helpful."

"Do you feel the need to talk about it? On the whole, men don't, do they? That's part of the problem."

Andrew wasn't sure whether Elaine was offering a friendly ear or whether she wanted to talk about her own situation. All he did know was that there were no circumstances under which he would have discussed Mary with anyone else. He stood looking at her, but saying nothing until the silence hung between them like a curtain. Elaine acknowledged this more rapidly than he did, and changed her tack, accordingly. She began talking about her own life and the weekend to come, how she always took the children to the Wolsey Theatre on Saturday afternoons and did the shopping while they were in their drama classes.

In the short time they spoke together, he became conscious of other teachers moving to their cars, thought of what Elaine had told him and felt angry. Why shouldn't they talk? It was quite nice standing close to a woman and simply listening to her concerns. Watching Elaine, he suddenly realised that he had always rather liked women. In fact, thinking about it, he recognised that all his closest friends were women – and that Mary had been the closest of all.

Elaine touched him on the sleeve as they parted – quite gently, as a mother might have done. She seemed unconcerned about how anyone passing might interpret her action, despite her earlier assertions about the swiftness with which gossip travels. It was a reassuring gesture as far as Andrew was concerned, and he perceived that it came from a lonely woman. It might well be that she needed to talk as much as he needed to listen.

"I must go," she said, "if you need to talk, or simply get out of yourself at any time – well, you know, a trouble shared is a trouble halved."

Without acknowledging why, and momentarily content within his own self-deception, Andrew found himself walking past the Wolsey Theatre on the following Saturday afternoon. He'd arrived in town early, and made his way straight to the theatre – to pick up a brochure in which he happened to notice that the children's drama classes ran from three until four.

He went back into the town centre, the brochure tucked into his pocket, and wandered among the dwindling number of bookshops, intent on finding something to read. His evenings were long, and he had found time for what once had been a favourite activity. He wanted a drink – not so much for the beer itself, but more for the simple pleasure of sitting quietly in a pub watching the world around him. Somehow, however, he didn't want the smell of alcohol on his breath. Eventually, Blends in the Buttermarket beckoned and he contented himself with a piece of chocolate fudge cake and a coffee, until it was time to drift back towards the Wolsey.

'Drift, wander, wonder, quietly': they were hardly dynamic words, were they? He smiled; it was only for a second, but it was reassuring, and he realised that he was looking forward to the afternoon. He had no reason to do so – no reason to suppose that he would actually meet Elaine, let alone that she would find time to have a drink with him. His being in town was not a sign of confidence, and certainly not of arrogance; he had no expectations other than that he would speak with her again.

It was she who saw him first, as she strode past Black Horse Lane towards the main town square. Her face lit up immediately, and Andrew's feelings were twofold – he was conscious of feeling safe and joyful: the sensation was all, and he did not think about it. Neither of their "hellos" feigned surprise, and he was pleased: a false emotion would have been a false start. She could do with something to eat – she and the children had only managed to "grab a snack" before they "dashed out". She thought Blends was nice, but – and he was relieved to hear this – but Café Nero closer.

Once the waitress had taken their order, Andrew said:
"You sound as though you've had a busy morning."
"I sound flustered, do I?"
"No – just busy."
"Yes – it has been a bit of a rush …"

She paused, and he knew that Elaine was wondering whether to go into the details of her hectic time. He could imagine the scene – children reluctant to get up, a week's housework to cover, ironing not done, no food in the fridge ... Elaine smiled, but said nothing – something he found unusual in a woman; Mary seemed to have made all the running as far as general chit-chat was concerned.

"How are the children, now," he enquired, "it's been – how long – eight months since Julian's death?"

"Yes," she answered, as apparently surprised at his question as he had been, "They only talk about it occasionally, and I never push the matter. As I said – when you were kind enough to lend me your ear – he had been gone for over two years. They loved their father, but they saw less and less of him as time went on. He wasn't part of their everyday lives, and ... he wasn't the man he had once been ... but you have your own problems, now, Andrew."

"Yes."

"It is best to talk about them – if you want to ... Not personal things, but those common to us all. How are you coping?"

He hadn't come to talk about his problems. He wasn't sure why he was with Elaine at all. He had the feeling that he simply wanted to be with a woman; he rather liked their company.

"I manage all right," he offered, by way of not wanting to appear too pleased with himself, "Domestically, I've always been independent, anyway, and – to be honest – it's much easier when you're alone."

"Less conflict about who does what, and what there is to be done? I expect you and Mary had your routines pretty well worked out, though?"

"Yes, we tended to know 'who did what', as you put it ..." he retorted, desperate that the conversation should not descend into a catalogue of domestic issues, "I find I have time on my hands now – which I didn't have before."

"You used to do a lot about the house?"

"Yes."

"I'd have hated that – Julian looked after the garden and car ... and so on, but I was 'Queen of the House'. That way, I knew where I was. I've been on my own a long time now, of course, and I've grown even more independent. I've always found that men need looking after. My father was the same as Julian. Do you cook?"

"Oh yes – I always have done. I enjoy it."

"Julian restricted himself to barbecues. It suited me that way. I've always enjoyed cooking. Somehow, I see that as the woman's role. My mother was the same. I enjoy family life. If Julian and I had remained together, I think another child may have been on the cards. I was getting broody ...You have the three, don't you?"

"Yes – after Amy arrived, we decided not to push our luck any further."

"Luck?"

"We had three healthy children. It seemed to be pushing our luck to go for a fourth."

"Oh, all children are a blessing ... whatever their health. I like children. I wish I'd had more."

"You obviously don't find it difficult – on your own," he opined, hoping to flatter her.

"No! I think children are better off with just a single parent than being involved in a contentious marriage.

I think the benefits of having a man around can be highly overrated," she laughed.

"We have our uses," replied Andrew, also laughing, he realised, for the first time in several weeks, "even if it's only to clean the car or do the garden."

"There's always the boy next door who could use more pocket money, or the old man down the road who needs something to do in his retirement."

He imagined that Elaine was being deliberately provocative, and knew that it was taking him out of himself. He laughed again.

"I think you need us more than we need you, Andrew."

That wasn't how Andrew felt, and such a view was in direct conflict with all his experience throughout his married life. He wondered how he and Elaine might have got on had they met earlier in their lives. He remembered something Mary had said about the Prices. 'I think she was rather wild … I think they had a good time. They … drank and ate with the best of them. They lived quite a gypsy life … before they settled down.' Andrew remembered the sense of loss he'd felt as he listened.

"Men need to sow their wild oats before they settle down," continued Elaine, as though touching on his innermost thoughts, "they're no good until they have. After that, you have to respect each other's differences. I didn't like Julian's family, particularly, but they were his family and it was easier to get on with them, than not. … I've never seen the point of arguing, and as long as you satisfy each other …"

She left the phrase hanging between them, but Andrew felt nonplussed. Her comment seemed to touch upon a sore point, but for whom he wasn't sure. Elaine seemed unperturbed, just as though she was making general conversation, applicable to no one in particular. When he said nothing, Elaine continued:

"Of course, you need to have similar social interests ..."

"And leave your work at school ..."

"Do teachers ever do that – I don't know of any. It's that kind of job ... Do you go to the theatre much, Andrew?" she said, suddenly, as though, he surmised, to deflect the conversation, which had flowed back into domestic issues.

"No, I can't say we do. Once you have children ..."

"Oh, you must leave time for yourselves – so many couples make that mistake – not leaving time for each other."

She seemed so wise and calm – a woman, despite all that had happened to her, at peace with herself. Andrew found the contentment and her independent spirit seductive. He was struck – recalling their meeting, later – with how different she had been when he met her after Julian's funeral, but at that time she had been talking about her children's reaction to their father's death. Perhaps, he surmised, Julian's funeral – terrible though the circumstances surrounding it had been – had brought for her what is commonly called 'closure'.

He looked at her across the table and was struck by the way her auburn hair hung in waves about her face, and dropped softly to her shoulders; he'd never noticed that before – not after work when they'd met at some course or other. They talked on, very comfortable in each other's company, until, abruptly, Elaine said:

"Look, I'm so sorry but the hour's gone. I must get back for the children – they're expecting me to be there ...We seem to have spent our time talking about me ... you're a good listener, Andrew. Perhaps another time, I'll listen to you," she laughed, although it seemed to Andrew that was exactly what she'd done.

CHAPTER 17

The past is always with us

"Andrew, you are coming to cut the grass, aren't you – I mean, you may have run out on us, but I can't be expected to do everything, can I?"

He'd picked up the phone to hear Mary's voice – not for the first time – on the other end of the line, and replied "I was under the impression that Jonathan was at home ..."

"Oh, you were under that impression, were you," she replied, although it wasn't a question, "He's gone away for a few days, visiting some old university friends."

"And he couldn't have cut the grass before he went?"

"He's a young man, Andrew. He's full of youth and zest for life. Most fathers don't expect their sons to cut their grass for them."

"He lives in the house, and makes full use of the facilities. Why shouldn't he share some of the chores," Andrew retorted, and – like Mary – he was making a statement of belief rather than posing a question.

He went, of course – what else could he do? After all, the grass did need cutting and, at least, his son wouldn't be there to hear any differences that might be aired.

When Andrew drew up on the roadside and got out of the car, the house beckoned him as it always had when he arrived home. He loved the house; it held so many of his memories. He'd been against buying an old place because he knew the cost involved in "bringing it up to scratch". (This was one of Mary's favourite phrases, although the cost was something she'd dismiss with a wave of her hand.) However, he had soon fallen in love with the very feel of what became 'home'. The frontage was small, and they had created a patio. It caught the morning sun, and they would often sit there, during the summer months, eating their breakfast, concealed from the road by the splash of red and green leaves of the red robin shrubs they had planted.

Mary was waiting, and opened the front door to him with a broad and welcoming smile. There was the vulnerability he remembered so well behind her smile, but it was, nonetheless, a welcoming one. She had cleaned the house to receive him. Andrew could smell the beeswax on the furniture, the polish on the tiles and the citrus-scented cleaner emanating from the partly-open door of the downstairs cloakroom. More enticing than any of these, however, was the aroma of fresh coffee brewing.

"I thought you might like a cup before you started," Mary said, leading him into the kitchen, "I'm just making it."

"Thanks."

"Is Madge all right?"

"Yes. I didn't think it a good idea to bring her back. I thought it might disorientate her."

"We all know the feeling. We rather miss her being here."

"I took her with me because no one else ever had time to exercise her, did they?" he remarked with what he knew to be a cutting edge, albeit a soft one.

Mary tightened her lips in another smile but said nothing. It was quite true; the expectation that he would walk, feed, groom and toilet the dog – despite the fact that she was a family pet – was endemic in the house. No one else ever moved from their chair if Madge whined at the door, but merely indicated that "Madge wants to go out."

"How are you?" enquired Mary.

"I'm fine, thanks," Andrew responded, not wishing to add "and you?", in case the talk became dialogue and they found themselves in the middle of a Noel Coward play; in that case, they would have both roared with laughter, and Andrew didn't want that – not at any cost.

Mary poured him a black coffee – just half a mug, which is the way he liked it – and placed a sweet biscuit on a tea plate by the side.

"You look rather drawn," insisted Mary, "Are you sure you're feeling well?"

"Yes, I'm fine."

"Aren't you interested in how I'm feeling?"

"Mary, I've come to cut the grass."

"But we need to talk."

"You need to talk. At the moment, I'm not ready for it. Now, just let me cut the grass," he persisted, desperate to get out through the kitchen door and into the garden.

"You can't deal with life by running away from it, Andrew."

"And you can't deal with it by talking about it incessantly."

"We have to talk sometime."

"We've spent our lives talking, and it has got us nowhere."

"Oh. I thought we'd had rather a successful marriage – in many respects."

He could see that she was widening the field of fire, and knew that soon there would be no cover. Verbal bullets would be flying everywhere. If he retaliated, it would only increase the harm done. He had learned – too late – that women enjoyed a "jolly good set-to", but it did nothing for him. It did not clear the air (as was so often claimed); it was neither 'jolly' nor 'good'.

"Look, I'll just cut the grass. OK?"

"No, it's not OK. I need to talk, and you ought to be prepared to talk if only for the children's sake. They need to understand what's going on, too."

It was strange that a couple who had been married so long, and had been so close, should now find the distance between them so apparently enormous. Both Mary and Andrew were aware of this, and both found it equally distressing.

"We need to see things as they are, Andrew, if we're to move forward, and I take it you do want to move forward, despite everything? You must know that this can't go on."

"I shouldn't have come today. It's quite clear that I'm not even going to leave the kitchen, let alone start up the lawnmower."

"Bugger the lawnmower," yelled Mary.

"It seemed important enough when you phoned," he said, trivialising the moment.

"Oh, don't be so silly ... There's no need to pull back from me, Andrew. I am your wife, and I do love you. You do know that? ... Well?"

"Yes."

"Then why can't we talk, and put things right? I don't want us to be unhappy, any more than you do. If this goes on, we could lose everything – home, family, everything. Isn't it worth making an effort to keep us together? All I want is for us to be with each other again – at peace – quiet, like we used to be. We built our own little world here. We made it a safe place – a haven to bring up the children – a home to which we could all retreat – away from the hustle and rancour of the world. How often have you come in at night and just thrown yourself down on the settee? How often have the children done the same? Everyone has always said what a happy home this is – a comfortable place to be. The children could always bring their friends here, and everyone was made to feel welcome. We created this world around them, Andrew – you and me."

"Then why aren't you content?"

"What? I am!"

"No, you're not. You are forever looking to 'improve' things, wondering what we can do next to 'make things better'."

"Aren't all women?"

"I don't know. I don't know all women, and I'm not given to drawing quick conclusions about people – women or men. What I do know is that we could live together forever – in this house or anywhere else – and you'd never be content with what we'd achieved. There would always be some way in which I could do something to improve things …"

"Oh, don't be so silly. Isn't everyone looking for ways to improve what they've got?"

"I don't know. I don't know everyone. And I'm not just talking about improvements to the house.

Nothing is ever quite good enough, is it? We finance – with great difficulty – one holiday a year, and suddenly find that someone else is taking two. We seem to be trotting along quite nicely, and discover that 'everyone else' is taking ballroom dancing lessons. When does it end – when we are, at last, at rest – and at peace – in our coffins?"

He'd never said as much before, although he had indicated his discontent – using humour – many times. She had taken it as "Andrew being Andrew", told him off when it had embarrassed her in front of friends, or laughed at him with the family, but never taken him seriously. He had even parodied himself for the amusement of others, as time went on.

Mary stared at Andrew, and he knew, before she opened her mouth, exactly what she was going to say.

"Do you know, sometimes, I don't think I've ever known you at all?"

The conversation went on for hours, round and round in interminable circles, and the grass was never cut. When Andrew finally escaped, by pretending to go to the toilet and then slipping out by the front door, he drove down to the Ipswich docks, crossed Stoke Bridge and eventually found his way, via the new road system, to the bottom of Bath Street. He got out and strolled to the edge of the Orwell.

Here, he had been a child: here, life had been simple – or so it had seemed to him at the time. Nothing in his childhood had prepared him for the verbal warfare of marriage. Had his grandparents kept their differences from the children, as he and Mary had done? He could not imagine that gentle old man ever arguing with his grandmother – although, come to think of it, she had a cold eye, which suggested a strong desire to have her way. Perhaps, by giving it, his grandfather had ensured the success of the marriage?

Had his parents followed suit? He could recall awful tensions between his parents, but they'd been sensed rather than apprehended; their cause had remained a mystery. This must be right, he kept telling himself; nothing could justify parents inflicting their grievances with each other upon their children. Yet, such a belief did not prepare you for marriage.

So what did – courtship? 'You and Mum went straight into marriage, didn't you? You never thought about it, did you? You just 'fell in love', and got married. My generation is going to be more careful. We're going to get to know each other first, and our marriages will be stronger for it.' He recalled his eldest son's words. It was true that the present generation of young people were not going into marriage blindly, simply because they fell in love. They were weighing the odds, calculating the chances of success, consolidating the relationship: would they be more successful for all that consideration? Andrew hoped so.

He looked down into the river. It was cleaner than when he was a boy, although he and his friends had swum in it safely enough with no adults to worry them. The water drifted past, making its way to the open sea, the gently-rippling waves drifting against each other in small, ambling eddies. It lapped the quayside, slap-slapping on the steps he remembered so well. They would sit there for hours, staring out across the river, wondering what they might find on the opposite shore. Despite knowing its dangers, Andrew had always found the river to be soothing. A strong, reckless swimmer he had drifted on its tides, swept along by its will, and never sensed the threat.

By the time he returned to his car, he felt at ease and drove along Wherstead Road towards the cottage he had selected as home.

Madge increased his sense of calm when she greeted him. After her walk, they sat in the garden, Andrew eating his smoked haddock on broccoli mash and 'Lady' – the nickname by which he always called her – curled over his feet. Realising the selfishness of the image he would have portrayed to an onlooker, Andrew laughed at himself; but the stillness was enticing – no one was going to find him something to do, and there would be no problems to solve or worries to which he had to listen for the rest of the evening.

He'd actually looked forward to the cut and thrust around the meal table – to their family togetherness at those times. They had always eaten together – as a family, round the table, with the television turned off – and they had talked, each contributing their own brand of wit to the occasion. Thinking back, he realised that Mary had often been the butt of much of the family humour, and the main contributors had been Jonathan and Amy. Robert had listened and chuckled, poking a little gentle fun at them all, while he, Andrew, had 'made the bullets for the others to fire', as Mary had once remarked.

The great thing was – there had been no animosity, and those times had forged their thoughts and beliefs as a family. Even during the teenage years, when Amy's views changed weekly – depending upon what was current wisdom among her friends at the time – Andrew had been aware of a consensus of agreement about basic convictions. Very different though they were – and Andrew had always hoped to forge three unique and independent adults from his children, each of whom would have the courage of their convictions – none of them had ever taken exception to the views of the others.

So why was it …? He refused to frame the thought, and then did. Why was it that Mary always took the opposite view to his over just about everything they discussed together – even when he knew full well that she actually agreed with his point of view? His father-in-law had once remarked "The irritating thing about women is that you know, they know, and they know you know – but they'll deny it!" Andrew had laughed at the time, not realising the implications.

He shook himself, and reflected further. Those times, and the many times they had loafed around together, had forged their identity as a family. Each of them knew their role within the family and in that knowledge there was safety – safety to experiment and grow without the risk of being ridiculed. The love between them was taken for granted, and pervaded the home.

It was while these thoughts rambled through his mind that the phone rang. He knew who it was because he had checked the voicemail when he arrived home. Mary had left several messages, saying how sorry she was they had argued, how she had only wanted to heal the rift between them and how she didn't know why she always ended up going over the same old ground. He ignored it. Andrew had spent nearly two hours at the house, and felt he'd had enough for one day.

The following day, Mary phoned him at school, apologising for having done so but insisting that she must speak with him and promising that she wouldn't "go on". Jonathan was going out with friends that evening, and so they would be free to talk. Would he bring Madge? Everyone missed her. Andrew wondered who would see her, since everyone was out, but he remained silent. He also wondered how Jonathan could afford to go out, but dismissed that thought as uncharitable.

When he arrived – without Madge for the reasons he'd already given – Mary once again had the house in pristine condition, with the addition of flowers in the lounge, hall and downstairs toilet.

"Mary", he proffered, quietly, before she had a chance to speak, "I'll give this conversation two hours and then I'm going – do you understand? They'll be no chasing me, screaming, when I leave the house. Is that agreed?"

The many times, following a couple of verbally bruising hours, she had pursued him into the garden, still yelling, were still very fresh in his mind. She flinched and flashed an angry look, although the anger found no voice.

"I don't think you need to take that tone, Andrew. All I want is a quiet conversation."

"Good – that's fine."

"Would you like a cup of tea?"

"No, I'll have a whisky, I think."

"Aren't you driving?"

"I'm having a standard double whisky – that is, 50 millilitres – two alcoholic units, which will have passed through my system during the two hours I am here. By the time I need to drive home, I will be free of alcohol."

"All right – there's no need to shout."

"I'm not shouting. I didn't raise my voice."

It was true. Acutely aware that Mary would accuse him of shouting – whether he had done so or not – Andrew had quite deliberately spoken in little above a whisper. Why did woman always do that – accuse you of shouting immediately you disagreed with them? He smiled to himself. The question was a stupid one; it was obvious why such accusations were a typical female ploy.

"What are you smiling at?" asked Mary.

"Nothing really: it would simply cause an argument if I told you."

Mary sighed; she, clearly, saw no point in chasing that line of discussion, and sat on the settee, while Andrew poured his drink and hers – a grapefruit juice topped with a slim-line tonic. He sat in the armchair, opposite her, and curled his legs over the arm.

"Won't you sit over here?" Mary enquired, tapping the cushion beside her.

He'd been in the room less than ten minutes and, already she had found fault with three things he had done – his choice of drink, his tone of voice and where he chose to sit: all of them a nonsense. Suddenly, Andrew felt relieved and he relaxed. He'd been right to do what he did; there was no reason on the face of the Earth why anyone should have to put up with such nit-picking – not once the children were grown into adulthood, and no longer dependent on the home.

"I've always found this chair to be very comfortable."

"If that's the way you want it."

There was a long pause in which Mary was either collecting her thoughts or containing her ... (disappointment?) ... at his tone of voice. She closed her eyes, but didn't sigh, and then began to speak, very softly.

"Andrew, I can understand how – at your age – you feel threadbare with life. You've got the responsibility of a very difficult job ..."

"I like my job – it's one of the great joys of my life."

"All right – but it does take a lot out of you. It's always on your mind. And you've got the family to worry about – getting the children through university ..."

"The children are not a problem. They'll take out their loans. By the time they have to pay them off, we'll have saved up enough to cover the tuition fees. I doubt whether we'll be able to cover the lot – especially if the Coalition gets its way – but it'll just leave them to pay the accommodation aspect of the loan. That's seems fair enough to me. If we'd only the one child, we might pay off everything."

"But you are fed up, aren't you? You're annoyed at Jonathan lounging about at home ..."

"Look, Mary, I don't see where this conversation is going. It's not the children with whom I have a dispute. Jonathan needs to get off his backside and find work – that's true – but we've argued about that, and you seem happy for him to be here ..."

"I'm not happy about it!"

"So why did you defend him when I raised the need for him to get a job?"

"He's my son."

"We're going round in circles again. Jonathan, Robert and Amy are not the issue – although your defence of Jonathan, whenever I raise the matter of his needing to find work, is one of them."

"My defence of Jonathan is an issue?"

"You're doing it again – deliberately taking the opposite point of view to mine, despite the fact that I know you think the same as I do, and have just said so."

"You're shouting again."

"Mary, Mary, quite contrary, how does your garden grow?"

Mary laughed. His singing of the nursery rhyme had always been a trigger point for laughter round the family meal table – in fact, his children usually joined in on the 'contrary'.

"Another drink?" asked Mary, quickly.

"No, I'd better not – I'm driving," he laughed.

"Come back," pleaded Mary.

His heart sank at the tone of her entreaty. It came from the heart, and he knew her well enough to accept its sincerity. He also knew that within a week Mary's other pre-occupations would have taken over, and that he would be the oil that kept her engine running, the safety valve that kept her boiler from blowing and the fuel that kept her turning over. He would very quickly assume his place very low down on her list of priorities. Andrew felt he could accept that provided he did not become the punch-bag for her grievances. Time and time again – argument after argument – he had found this not to be possible.

"At least come back for the summer. We can deny you ever left – confound the gossips. I won't crowd you, Andrew. I won't put pressure on you …"

'Until the grass needs cutting – and *can't* be left but *must* be done – ready for the next barbecue,' he thought, but said nothing. He could hear her voice rising, insistent with the hysterical fear that their friends might find the grass was too long.

"If it doesn't work out, then I'll let you go – if that's what you want. I promise. Just give it a try …"

That word 'just' again! God, how he hated that word 'just' – always spoken as though he'd 'just' done that one thing for her in all their life together: spoken as though nothing else he had ever done counted or mattered. In extreme moments of consideration, he wondered whether the word 'just' had ever driven men to murder: that, certainly, would be 'a crime of passion'.

"I can understand that you might want your freedom," she continued, lifting her eyes to look him full in the face, "I can understand that marriage isn't easy ... I know your sensitivities, Andrew – I know the things you want to do with your life ... and I don't want to stand in your way. I love you too much for that ... I know you take things to heart that other men shrug off – and I love you for it. It's one of the things that attracted me to you in the first place. I couldn't, anyway, be happy knowing that I was holding you back. What sort of future would we have, my being so selfish ...?"

"You're not selfish, Mary ..."

"Let me finish, Andrew. I need to say this while it's clear in my head ... I've wanted us to be quiet and peaceful enough for me to say this for a long time. When two people love each other – and I do know we love each other – then they should be prepared to give each other the freedom each of them needs ... I wouldn't stand in your way ... but let us keep the family together ... there is no need for a divorce. In the end, it will solve nothing for either of us."

Andrew had always been astounded at the wisdom of women; they seemed to be in touch with truths that eluded men. There was magnanimity in her thoughts that could only earn his respect, and the evening concluded – when he left, quietly and after a kiss – with a kind of peace having been wrought between them.

CHAPTER 18

Turning back the clock

Andrew just happened to be in town the following Saturday when he bumped into Elaine Price: he was sure of this – sure that no duplicity was intended. He had driven to town early, hoping to happen upon a novel (he was reading much more these days), and found himself sitting in the sun outside Blends enjoying a black coffee and an Eccles cake when Elaine came walking along the Buttermarket.

As she approached, he noticed for the first time what she was wearing and the colour of her hair – things he was suddenly aware that he had never noticed before. He hadn't realised how dark her hair was, or how red suited her colouring.

"How are your hanging baskets?" she asked, with a smile that seemed mischievous.

"Blooming: provided I remember to water them. This dry weather does flowers no good at all ..." He was about to add that, had he still been at home, Mary would have reminded him, as soon as he walked in or while they were eating dinner, that the garden needed watering, but he thought better off it and said, instead, "Would you like a latte... and ... what was it? ...a piece of carrot cake?"

"Fancy you remembering that," she responded, warmly.

He almost said "habit", but – once again – held his tongue, and signalled to the waitress who took Elaine's order.

"What are you reading?"

"*Bleak House* – it's years since I read Dickens, and I thought it would be good to get lost in a novel. I've always liked long stories, and I suddenly find that I have time for reading."

"I never found that to be one of the benefits of being single, but then I had the children with me … It must be quite nice to 'get lost'. I always enjoyed that about reading when I was younger. I can remember my parents getting really irritated when I didn't want to leave a book to eat my dinner."

"'You've always got your nose stuck in a book' – is that what they said? Oh for the old days when books were the main distraction for children. It certainly brought on their reading. Do yours read much?"

"Yes, fortunately, but then I'm strict about how much TV they watch."

"Amy was a big *Harry Potter* fan and Jonathan was into science fiction, but Robert always preferred factual books. He's the kind of boy who might one day re-write encyclopaedias."

"Do you miss them?"

"Yes. I think it was quite a wrench when Amy – she's the youngest – left to go to university. Even though they come back for the holidays – and Jonathan's at home now – it isn't quite the same. They're never really there – if you know what I mean."

"No – but I haven't experienced that yet. The idea of losing them is more than I can bear to think about."

"If you could just keep them young – pre-pubescent – and freeze your life like that forever, it would be wonderful, but 'the moving finger writes and, having writ, moves on' …"

"Oh, don't. It's one thing you can never do – turn back the clock. I learned that – Julian and I learned that – very quickly."

Andrew, whose mind had been on his children, looked up from his Eccles cake, sharply. It was obvious that the strain of their conversation had struck a discordant note with Elaine. She hesitated, looked at him quietly and then continued.

"He left us in the summer – just as the summer holiday started. I don't think he could bear the thought of six long weeks with me – or maybe it was her not wanting six weeks without him – who knows? Anyway, the first time we got together after that was on Rosemary's birthday, which is in September. It was meant to be a happy occasion – the four of us going to Pizza Hut, which was somewhere the children had always loved … It was so tense. It's unbelievable how tense it was. You know how families talk – in-jokes, teasing each other, arguing in that special way? Well, it was nothing like that – the talk didn't flow as it had when Julian was their dad and living at home. It was just awkward – that's the only word for it … and the children noticed, too – it wasn't just me – because they mentioned it afterwards.

He left us when the meal was over and went back to her, while the children and I went home. I realised, as I sat thinking about it after the children were in bed, that those times – our family times – had gone forever. There'd be no more lolling around in each other's company, no more laughter of the family kind, no more shared past. Julian had broken the thread of our unity. He'd destroyed the ... the ease we had – the banter, the fun. From then on, whenever we got together, it was going to be tortuous. It was going to be overwhelmed by regret and a sense of loss."

Elaine, whose eyes had been fixed on some point beyond Andrew's head, looked down at him as she continued, "Make no mistake about it, Andrew, the effects of a divorce are devastating."

"You mean you wish that you were ...," began Andrew, realising as he did so that there was no longer a choice for Elaine, "I mean, during those two years when ... Julian was with ... with ... her ... During that time, you wished you were back together?"

"I wish it had never happened. I don't know that ... after you've been betrayed ... that you can get back together ... Julian changed in those two years. He wasn't the man he had been, and I don't think he ever would have been again ... I do know that the family was torn apart, and that trying to pretend it wasn't with family get-togethers – like Rosemary's birthday – was not realistic. It had a touch of ... hypocrisy about it – as though everyone was pretending that everything was all right. Do you see what I mean?"

"Yes, I think so."

They sat in silence for some time. Andrew ordered a second coffee – although Elaine declined his offer of another – and she took her carrot cake apart, slowly. He became aware that they were very comfortable in each other's company; he had no idea why, only accepting that it was unusual. He had the feeling that he was being of some use. Suddenly, Elaine laughed: it was an unnatural sound and broke the harmony between them.

"It's not a popular view," she offered.

Andrew considered it to be an explanation for her mirth, but said nothing. He sipped his coffee and waited.

"It's not one that wins me any rosettes for saying it in company. Everyone likes to think that it's all for the good, and regrets aren't allowed. It's natural, I suppose, for people to want to view the decisions they make in a positive light, isn't it? Who is going to admit that they have failed – that the decision to divorce was the wrong one? Nevertheless, I'm sure that many people do regret such a decision, and wish that they had stayed in their marriages, however … imperfect they might have been."

Elaine looked at her watch – suddenly aware that time was moving on – and then looked at Andrew with a smile that might have been sad, or simply resigned.

"People are not honest about divorce, you see, Andrew. They say whatever they think other people want to hear, or whatever preserves the status quo despite the fact that the status quo no longer exists … You need to be very sure about what you are doing."

"You never divorced, did you?"

"No – but the split was made. It was a divorce in all but name."

"And Julian felt that, too?"

"I wasn't sure that I was talking about Julian," she replied, with a pointed look at him, "but you're probably right. Yes, he might well have regretted it, after it was too late. What he had with her was second best. His real loyalties were with me and the children, and he might have come to realise that ..." Elaine's voice tailed off, and she swigged down the remains of her coffee. "I have no doubt that Julian did want a divorce – at first – but divorce isn't simple, as I've said. It has repercussions that last forever. We were going through some difficult years, and he thought he'd make a fresh start. He thought it would solve all his problems, but it didn't. You can't cut the knot of family ties, and that was something he never understood ... At the same time, once the break is made, you can't go on pretending – no more 'happy family birthdays' ... or 'merry Christmases' ... Look, I must go. The children will be out of their classes soon, and there're one or two things I must pick up. I'm so sorry, Andrew – we seem to be part-way through a conversation. I didn't expect to see you here, and you got me talking. Thanks for listening. How much ...?"

"That's OK – I'll see to the coffees. It's nice to have had a chat."

"Thanks. Bye."

Watching her scurrying further along the Buttermarket and turning right down Upper Brooke Street, Andrew realised that she must have been going to Wilkinson's, which had a reputation for inexpensive household goods. He also realised that she hadn't been talking about Julian, and wondered at her wisdom and her prudence.

He was fully aware that he had not really discussed the matter with Mary, and knew there was no way that he could. Whenever he had hinted at any dissatisfaction with just about anything, she had always become hysterical. It was then the anger would surface and the hissing would become a squall that broke over them.

He supposed that she had always been like it – brushing off, in that fearful way of hers, any suggestion that things between them were not perfect. Thinking back, he recalled the violent rows between Mary, her elder sister, Elspeth, and their mother; thinking back, he realised that – in order to expiate their differences – the three women had always turned, in the end, on the father. He wondered whether her way of dealing with frustrations had been learned in childhood. The father had always soaked up the abuse, and retreated to the pub. Perhaps retreat was the only answer – that, or to learn to live with the spillage.

Andrew knew that he could not live in that way. He had not expressed in words (even to himself) the steps that led him to the decision to consult a solicitor; at the end, the 'decision' had been intuitive – perhaps, quite simply, a final exasperation. Should he have taken up the solicitor's offer to consult Relate – whoever Relate were? He thought not. His was not a generation that had too much faith in counselling. If two intelligent people could not sort out their own problems, then what hope had a stranger? Anyway, how would either Mary or he begin to express their feelings about their relationship: the very thought seemed like a betrayal.

Perturbed by what Elaine Price said, Andrew had wondered into Christchurch Park and now stood, leaning on the metal railings, watching the ducks. He was near home – he knew that – and almost hoped that Mary might stroll through the park, and that they would bump into each other. They might, then, begin to talk as they had once done, when young and when the world was easily put to rights. They had even laughed at her father's retreats to the pub as being no way to face up to his problems. It hadn't occurred to Andrew that the problems had not been the old man's, but those of the women in his life.

He knew he was trying to talk himself round to a return. If Elaine was right, a return would be simpler. He really could not bear the thought that there would be no more 'family occasions'; the idea had not occurred to him. Mary had said that he would never spend another Christmas with his children because she would see that he didn't – but that was Mary, not his children – not his three, independent-minded children.

He knew that they would be hurt by the divorce, but rather thought they would understand – or, at least, accept that he had acted in good faith. He could not really believe that three people who he loved, and upon whom he had expended so much time and energy and care would turn their backs on him. If that were the case, then surely there would be 'family occasions'. He and Mary were civilized people. Surely they could sit down together with their children – even after a divorce – and share a meal, a family event, an occasion?

Andrew was a listener, and had never heard anyone suggest that divorce split families, irrevocably and forever, until Elaine Price had said her piece. He knew a number of divorced people, and they seemed happy enough – a happiness that would not be conceivable if they were at loggerheads with their families. He had no time for the platitude of the 'clean break'. People who held that view were simply shallow, and did not value their past. His family did, and it would continue into their futures – divorce or no divorce.

It had not occurred to him that people lied about divorce, but – if Elaine was right – then the only inference he could draw was that those people to whom he had listened were not being truthful, and that the pain of divorce did reverberate throughout the rest of their lives. Were there people who dare not face the truth of what they had done, and lived in a continual deceit about themselves? Were they afraid to admit that they might, in some respects, have made a mistake? If these people missed their old family life, why couldn't they be honest about it? No decision in life was ever going to be completely 'right': there would always be the pros and the cons.

No answers came: the thoughts were beyond his experience. He was struggling, in the light of Elaine's honesty, with his own fears for his family. Something told him, however, that there was validity in making a return. You cannot turn back the clock. The habits of behaviour towards each other that married couples developed in the early years could not be unravelled: within a week of his walking through the door, the attitudes which beset him would, once again, be in place – and he would resent them.

Andrew left the ducks to their play and walked from the park, past the old gate-keepers lodge, out through the little gate that swung around its centre bar and into the freedom of the town.

CHAPTER 19

The birthday party

The term had still a month to go; the work was hectic and the atmosphere in school was high. The May Day celebrations had gone with a swing, but parents' evenings were just round the corner, there were reports to write and sports day was looming. The weather was dry and sunny and wonderful for the children, but it was an energy-sapping time for the staff.

Another letter from his solicitor lay on the doormat when Andrew arrived home on June 21st; it was just three months since he had provided her with the grounds for the divorce, and Mary had fought against it every step of the way. His younger son, Robert, had also left a message on his voicemail: could he come round to see him that evening? If he didn't hear to the contrary, he'd be there at about half-past six. Andrew looked at his watch. It was six o'clock already, and the tone of Robert's voice suggested something serious. Andrew thought of the date, and its significance was not lost on him: today was going to be a long one.

Andrew was pan-frying two gammon steaks in cider, when he heard a car pull onto the gravel driveway followed by Robert's gentle knock on the front door. The expression on his son's face when Andrew opened the door did nothing to alleviate his feelings of foreboding. Madge relieved the moment, in her excitement at seeing Robert again.

"A mate dropped me off, dad. Will you be OK to take me back?" said Robert, by way of explanation as to how he had arrived. When Andrew smiled an affirmative, Robert disappeared for a moment, with Madge at his heels. Andrew heard him mumble "thanks" and then his younger son joined him in the kitchen. 'So organised,' thought Andrew, 'it's almost frightening. Better a friend than an enemy.'

"I assumed you hadn't eaten," he said to Robert, "and I certainly haven't. It's gammon in cider, and I've done potatoes mashed in mustard to go with it." He knew, full well, how much his son enjoyed meat – especially pork.

"I have, actually – mum got home early this evening," laughed his son, fondling the ears of the dog, "but I can always handle another meal, and I'd never say no to gammon."

"Well, pour yourself a cider, and toss those peas into that pan of boiling water, will you? I'm sorry it's peas. I didn't have time to prepare the purple sprouting broccoli."

"I'm surprised at you, dad. I thought you were better organised."

"Yes ... I didn't get in until six. We're not all university students on three months holiday," he replied, to Robert's chuckle.

They ate in relative silence, comfortable in each other's company. Andrew drew no conclusions from this: throughout his life he had noticed that men do not seem to need to converse, continually, to feel at ease.

He had once enjoyed a longish car journey, with his eldest son, on their way to a concert under the aegis of 'Music in Country Churches'. Jonathan had been driving, and they had passed only the occasional remark, but this hadn't detracted from their enjoyment of each other's friendship at all.

When the meal was over, however, and Andrew had replenished their glasses of cider, Robert looked at his father and said: "Ye-es, dad." He had a way of drawing out his speaking of the word 'yes', whenever he had something important to say. "It's about my twenty-first birthday bash."

"Go on," replied Andrew, knowing what his son was about to say, and how awkward it was going to be for him.

"Well, we're having a sort of barbecue in the garden at home – family, mum's friends, mates – that sort of thing, you know – nothing special …"

'Just about everyone you or we have ever known,' thought Andrew, but contained his view – not wishing to embarrass his son. Instead he said "I didn't realise you were having a do at all, Rob. I thought we did the coming-of-age thing at your eighteenth."

"Yes, we did, but mum thought we ought just to mark the occasion. It's just Auntie Elspeth, Uncle Brian and their family and a few of my mates from school."

"And our friends – your mum's and mine?"

"Yes."

"Sounds nice. Your birthday is on the Wednesday, isn't it – so I take it that the barbecue is on the – what …?"

"The 30th of July. Mum will have broken up by then."

Andrew looked at his son, wondering how he could help him through the next phase of their conversation.

"You see, dad …" Robert began, and looked at his father across the table.

"Your mum would rather I didn't come?"

"Yes – I'm sorry, but she thinks it would be embarrassing."

"I see."

"What I came to say was – how about us taking a weekend away to mark my eighteenth. We could go walking – have a few beers – that kind of thing. I think Jon would be up for it. I don't know about Amy."

"Rob – is this how it's going to be – two birthday celebrations each time – one for everyone else and another for me? Will the three of you have two weddings – two christenings for each of any children you might have?"

"There's no need to be like that, dad. You know what mum's like. She thinks they'll be tension if you're there … Uncle Brian has already made it clear that he doesn't want to speak to you again …"

'But this is your birthday, Rob,' thought Andrew, 'You're my son. Are Uncle Brian's views and feelings more important than mine? And this is your celebration – surely you want me there? Can't everyone just accept what's happened as none of their business, and concentrate on helping you enjoy your barbecue?' Afterwards, Andrew came to the conclusion that he should have spoken his thoughts but, at that moment, he saw only that he would be making things more difficult for his son.

He could imagine how strung-up Mary would have been as the family discussed the possibility of the barbecue, how aware she would have been of how acutely embarrassing it would be to have him present: the air in the family home would have reeked with her tension. Sitting in his kitchen, Andrew could smell the sweat of the nervous stress in the air. He walked over to the back door and opened it. Mary's fear of "what other people will think" had dominated their social lives: so much so that certain topics of conversation had been almost ritually banned when they were in company. Whenever Andrew had 'transgressed', hours of vitriolic de-briefing of his behaviour had followed. Had he been foul-mouthed when voicing his opinions or fascist in his views, Andrew could have understood her concern (no, her 'anguish' would be a word nearer the truth), but neither of these were applicable to his style of conversation. 'Do I dare to eat a peach?' Eliot's line came back to him. He might have lived his whole life saying only what his wife thought others wanted to hear. 'Freedom – what a price you demand,' he thought, but turned to his son with a smile.

"OK, Rob. A weekend's walking sounds great to me. How about the White Peak area of Derbyshire – Miller's Dale, Tideswell, Stanton, Youlgreave? They all bring back memories."

Memories, that was, of family holidays they had taken when the children were young. Andrew had realised, some years before, that his 'children' were at an age when recalling childhood memories was embarrassing, and Rob's cry of "da-ad" had sometimes silenced such reminiscing; but this evening his son seemed pleased to talk and they recalled family times past.

One occasion, in particular, had always brought much laughter – especially when they were very young.

Sitting outside a pub (washed and ready for bed, with their pyjamas on under their day clothes), on a typically wet camping trip, Andrew had encouraged each of them to "take a sip, but only a sip" of his beer. The 'sips', of course, had grown into gulps as each child took their turn until – amid roars of laughter – Andrew's pint had virtually disappeared down their young throats.

Robert, like his father, had always enjoyed family get-togethers, but more as a listener than a talker; his contributions came as one-off remarks that spurred on the conversation. Once he began talking, however, his reminiscences became reflective and his conversation both informative and stimulating. It was like that on this particular evening, as they sat in Andrew's garden, watching the sun go down and drinking cider.

By the time it was dark, they had both consumed too much alcohol to even consider Andrew driving his son home, and so Robert stayed the night in the spare bedroom. As Andrew fell into a troubled sleep, he realised that – much as he had enjoyed the evening – more had been left unsaid than shared; but they had agreed a date for the Peak District weekend.

It was over two weeks later – with the end of term in clear view – that Amy turned up on his doorstep, having caught a couple of buses to reach him; the birthday barbecue was still three weeks away.

"I'm sorry I didn't get here before, dad," she said, petting Madge and steering the excitable leaps away from her legs as she spoke, "I don't know where the time goes. Rob said you were upset, and I tried to get round earlier."

"Sit down. You've chosen a good morning – Saturday. I've nothing to do. After this dry spell even the grass doesn't need cutting. I'm just about to make a coffee. How do you like it – black in a chipped mug?"

"Not unless I'm pretending to be a student – although we did have baked beans for breakfast. Is all this ... stuff yours?"

"No – the cottage came furnished. I think it's a holiday home. Your mum had baked beans for breakfast?"

"No. I cooked them for Tristan and me. He's staying at the moment. We're off to France in a couple of weeks – backpacking."

"Very nice, too," said Andrew, thinking how difficult it must be for Mary to have a guest in the house so near the end of term, thinking how selfish it was of Amy to have imposed one at such a time and realising he was pleased not to be caught in the middle. He could hear Mary going on and on about it, without actually wanting him to say or do anything.

"Things are pretty busy at home, then?"

"Bit hectic," she replied, catching the tone of her father's comment, "but Tristan's only one more mouth to feed. Mum doesn't mind."

Andrew placed a cappuccino on the table in front of Amy and, picking up a tin of shortbread biscuits, suggested that they sat in the garden.

"You still make a good coffee, then, dad?"

"I was lucky. They have an excellent machine here. I was very grateful."

"Why don't you come back?"

"Is that what you've come to say? I thought you said Robert was upset, and I took it that you'd come without Tristan so that we could talk about why?"

"Tristan's in town with Jonathan. We don't have any secrets from each other. It's a pity your generation don't share things more. Maybe then you wouldn't get yourselves into such a mess."

"You would have preferred it if your mother and I had shared our differences with you and your brothers?"

"Sometimes people need to talk, dad. You can't bottle everything up."

"There are some things that parents cannot discuss with their children ... and, even if they could, it is not always possible to put your finger on what the grievance is – at the time. You must have heard people say they 'wonder what the argument was all about'."

"Yes ..."

"Besides, your mum and I did not row as such ... did you ever hear us?"

"No."

"And you'd rather you had? You'd rather have carried that emotional load around with you?"

"No ..."

Andrew was shutting off avenues of dissent. He knew that, and could not stop himself; but he did not want to have a row with his daughter. A word spoken exists for the rest of your life. There is no way that it can ever be retracted, and the umbrella of anger gives no excuse. He was behaving with his daughter as he had dealt with Mary's outbursts: closing them down, shutting them off, and preventing that awful outburst of explosive steam. He looked at her across the patio table and smiled.

"I'm sorry," he said, "I just do not want to fall out with you. What is Robert upset about – apart from the obvious?"

"You're doing it, again, dad. You're stating the case, and closing it down – on your own terms, in a way you can understand."

"I'm sorry. I'm listening."

"Robert wants you at his birthday barbecue, but he doesn't want mum upset. He wants you to know that … dad?"

"I'm sorry, I thought you had more to say. I do know that."

"But you didn't tell Robert that you understood."

"He must have known. We parted on good terms. We agreed our walking weekend."

"We don't know why you've left, dad. You never told us."

"It's between me and your mum."

"She showed me the reasons on your divorce petition."

"She did what!"

"She had to talk to someone …"

"Then you know."

"Mum being dissatisfied with just about everything – you being low on the list of her priorities – hemmed in by social dos and don'ts – going on and on about her work – regular outbursts of verbal abuse – you never up to the mark – antagonistic to your side of the family … dad, those aren't reasons!"

"They aren't?"

"No."

"I see … I didn't want to … I really cannot talk about this with you, Amy."

"You didn't want to put anything more personal? After all, what you said must apply to just about every couple under the sun, mustn't it?"

"Must it?"

"Dad, don't keep repeating everything I say. It's irritating."

"Sorry," replied Andrew, thinking it must have been the fourth or fifth time he'd said that, and wondering for what he was apologising – except his point of view. He looked at his daughter for whom he felt nothing but love. "Another coffee?"

"Thanks."

Andrew took his time making the coffee, and wished he'd bought some muffins, or made some scones, to go with it; they were the little considerations that women thought about more than men. He offered Amy another shortbread biscuit with her second cappuccino.

"Your generation went into marriage head-first, didn't you," she stated, without any hint of a question in her voice, despite the phrasing, "It was a crash course in intimacy for you, wasn't it? I've seen those 60s films and the attitude to sex is always the same: the woman's always gagging for it, always receptive to it and always fulfilled by Mr Wonderful. I know the Bonds and Carry-ons were mass entertainment, but those using Lawrence's material should have known better – and so should he. What he knew about women could be written on the back of a postage stamp."

"Jonathan said much the same ... only in rather less words," replied Andrew, wondering whether his daughter was speaking for herself or on behalf of some university lecturer's re-appraisal of 60s' cinema and its influence on social behaviour. Perhaps, he thought, 'social intercourse' might be a more appropriate phrase, using 'intercourse' in its rather narrow current meaning and not as Jane Austen might have used it. He said as much to Amy.

"You're being defensive again, dad."

"I'm 70s – not 60s."

"You're doing it again. Besides, we are always more influenced by the cinema of the previous decade. They're the films we see on television as children."

"I respect your views, Amy, and I do understand what you're suggesting, but you're wide of the mark."

"Am I?"

"Yes."

"Dad – mum received a letter."

"A letter?"

"Yes. We know all about the 'other woman'. We even have a detailed description of her ..."

Andrew's heart sank as he listened to his daughter recounting the arrival of an anonymous letter that had "pulled the carpet from under mum's feet". Evidently, Mary had opened it, burst into tears and fallen back on the settee. Amy, Robert and Jonathan joined her, and the letter had been read by the three of them. The letter had included a detailed description of Elaine Price – the writer even seemed to know where she lived – and a denunciation of men in general; it appeared that the writer's husband (yes, the anonymous correspondent was a woman) had left her for another woman and returned when 'the affair' didn't work out. The 'reconciliation' had been anything but, and the writer was never able to trust her husband again; whenever he left the house – even if it was only to get a packet of cigarettes – she couldn't be sure where he was going.

"And you believe all this?" enquired Andrew when Amy had finished.

"Do you deny it, dad?"

"That's not what I asked. Do you believe the writer of the letter?"

"Is there any reason we shouldn't?"

"I'll try again, since you're only answering my questions with further questions – something, I believe, you've accused me of in the past. Do you believe what was in the letter with regard to Elaine Price and me?"

"It's a well-known syndrome, dad, for men of your age. Seventy per cent of men in your generation have affairs."

"But it won't happen in your generation because you're getting to know each other well first. You're starting out on a firmer foundation, and your marriages will be stronger for it?"

"There's no need to be sarcastic, dad."

"Do you think for one moment that your mum and I didn't believe that, too – when we got married?" replied Andrew, leaving the table as he spoke, and ambling towards the end of the small garden. "You still haven't answered my question. Do you believe …?"

"I heard what you said, and yes I suppose we did."

"So there is more truth in an anonymous letter written by an embittered woman than in what I have said?"

"It isn't quite like that …"

"It's exactly like that … we all make our choices in life, Amy, and you – and your brothers and mother – have just made one of yours."

"Dad, you didn't tell us anything."

"You specifically asked me whether there was another woman, and I said that there was not. As regards the reasons for the divorce, your mother has shared those with you – something I would not have done – and you've dismissed them as being no reasons at all. So it would have been pointless my sharing them, anyway."

"You're not living at home, dad! You're not having mum going on and on about her not understanding why it happened. You do not have to listen to her raving about 'that woman'!"

"Dead right: now, do you begin – in the wisdom of your youth – to understand?"

In the disarming way she always had about her, Amy came over and put her arms round her father. They said little more about which they could argue; the disagreements had cut quite deeply enough. They talked generally, gradually bringing the tension down so that they could part as friends – and as father and daughter – rather than two strangers. He learned of her and Tristan's plans to harvest grapes in France, and wondered if they'd checked the date; he said nothing because his intervention would not have been considered helpful. He told her to reassure Robert that he was not offended, and was looking forward to their walking holiday. Amy apologised for not being able to join them, but thought that Jonathan might. He also told her that Elaine Price had been maligned in the letter and that this was not fair; on that point, they agreed to differ.

Later, he drove her back into Ipswich where she was to meet her boyfriend. He watched her walking away from the car, thought of how she had all her life in front of her and wondered when he would see her again.

CHAPTER 20

The intimacies of conversation

Andrew came as near to his son's barbecue as he was able. Walking Lady in Christchurch Park and then along the Tuddenham Road brought him within smelling distance of the occasion; he contented himself with a pint of Adnams' Explorer in The Woolpack, and then made his way home.

It was a week later when he received a phone call at work from his sister-in-law, Elspeth. Would he meet her for lunch one day? Would he be sure not to mention this to anyone because Brian – her husband – would be furious if he knew? Yes – he would, and yes – he would be sure.

Andrew had always been on friendly terms with his sister-in-law. Jonathan had explained the psychology of this to him, but the thinking was rather lost on Andrew: as far as he was concerned they "just got on". Elspeth worked at the Ipswich Hospital on Heath Road, and so he suggested the Golf Hotel that was nearby for both of them. Occasionally this was used by his staff, but never midweek: primary school teachers did not take lunch breaks during the week – the time was needed to prepare the practical side of the afternoon sessions. He also knew that Elspeth delighted in being something of a snob and that she would have a few caustic remarks to make about the menu, the fact that this was a family pub and that it was "a tad down-market". She did not disappoint him – 'The Mexican', 'The Indian' and 'The Hawaiian' played straight into her hands, with the slogan 'Great food, honest value' adding the icing on the 'chocolate fudge cake'.

"Hmm – you certainly know how to treat a girl, Andy," Elspeth quipped, turning the laminated menu over as though she was clearing up after her cat.

"We have a quiet spot by the window …" he pleaded.

"Overlooking the plastic climbing frames …"

"And with a 2 for 1 offer on steak and chips," he suggested.

"I see the tomato sauce comes in those vulgar little sachets," she continued.

"Are you telling me your class of person prefers those horrible, messy bottles?"

The conversation drifted through the usual topics of in-laws – the children, the social life, the forthcoming holidays, what was being done to the house … – until, suddenly, Elspeth steered it forward, with a hard laugh.

"So you've left the fold, then?" she said.

"Yes, I suppose I have."

"There's no suppose about it – you have. You must have realised how embarrassing that would be for Mary," she challenged, laughing again. Mary's embarrassment at any social faux pas was a standing joke between the four of them, and Elspeth's remark indicated no concern; she found her sister's humiliation rather amusing. Andrew felt that she saw in it a certain triumph on her own part.

"She wants you back, you know."

"You've not come at …"

"You didn't expect Mary would ask me to come, did you?"

"No. It was just a sudden thought," he answered, realising the stupidity of the idea: under no circumstances would Mary have asked her older sister to intervene. She had always felt that their marriage was in many respects superior to Elspeth's and Brian's.

"All marriages hit their rocky patches you know," Elspeth pursued, "it hasn't always been milk and honey for Brian and me." She paused and laughed on the phrase 'milk and honey' indicating, he thought, that it had never been so, and that Andrew's expectation that marriage should be was naïve.

"You've seen me in a state," he said, quietly, recalling for her an evening when she and Brian had arrived to find him in tears and Mary raging around the garden. "'It can't go on like this' – I think that's what you said."

"Your expectations of marriage are naïve, Andrew. You knew what she was like when you married our Mary … What do you hope to find …" asked Elspeth, and then added "… on the other side of the hill?"

"Some people relish conflict – I can understand that – the verbal cut and thrust of marriage is what they want – but I don't."

"It's always fun making up afterwards."

"Rubbish – and you know it," he snapped, "That's just a cliché to make an excuse for bad temper."

Andrew looked at his sister-in-law as he spoke. She was far away, remembering things she shared with no one. The waiter arrived with Andrew's steak and chips, and Elspeth's healthy tuna, bean and onion salad. "Can I get you anything?" asked the waiter.

"Yes," replied Elspeth, when he had gone, "You can get under a bus."

"He was only asking," laughed Andrew.

"That's what I say to Brian, sometimes – when we've had a row and he's trying to make up. 'I'm going to the shops,' he'll say, 'Can I get you anything?' And that's my reply … I don't mean it, of course … well, not always … he hasn't kissed me, you know – not properly, not for nearly twenty years."

It was at such moments that Andrew felt totally inadequate. What was there to say? Had he offered sympathy, Elspeth would have bitten his head off, not wanting to acknowledge any fault in her marriage.

"You have to learn to take the rough with the smooth, Andrew. That's what life – and marriage – is all about … Is your steak all right?"

"Fine – and your tuna salad?"

"Healthy … She'll have no one to talk to, Andrew. You've always been there for her. She shares everything with you: every grief, every happiness. She worries when you're late back from work or if you haven't walked the dog on time. Who is she going to talk to about the children? Women might share those concerns with another woman, but it's not the same. No one else has that special interest in your family. She's going to feel shut off – isolated – not only from you but from everyone else. She'll turn in on herself. It'll become unbearable … for the children."

Elspeth looked up from her salad, and Andrew thought she felt she'd said too much.

"How do you think she'll feel having no one to check the doors at night, or clear away the supper things?" she added, with a laugh.

"I can see what you mean," he replied in what he hoped was a conciliatory tone, but which actually sounded lame.

"So what are you going to do about it?"

There was nothing to say in response to her bluntness; he saw no middle path. He ate his steak, and every bite seemed dry: though the meat was succulent and well-cooked, it cleaved to his mouth.

"You are well, aren't you?"

"Yes."

"Not depressed?"

"No."

"You've always been a bit on the thoughtful side. It's not always good for you."

"I've always been somewhat melancholic, if that's what you mean."

"That's just a fancy way of saying 'depressed'. It doesn't help to romanticise. You can get help, Andy."

"Counselling?"

"Your tone says it all. Our generation don't 'do' counselling, do we? Perhaps we should ... I don't want to pry into your feelings – although you're not as much of a closed book as you think – but if this goes on, you'll lose everything. You'll get so far apart there'll be no way back."

"I'm listening."

"No, you're not. You're hearing what I say, but you're not listening. I'm not trying to pry into your feelings – some things are best left alone. Brian always said you and Mary spent too much time talking about each other's feelings, and that you'd be better off just getting on with it – but that's Brian ... He had a point, though."

Elspeth shared her husband's beliefs, thought Andrew, and yet felt obliged to put him down. Why? Her thoughts about Brian seemed to trigger Elspeth's memory because she gave her rather arch little smile and began talking about Mary again.

"Brian and she have always got on well, haven't they? I sometimes think he'd have been better off marrying her. She's his type in many ways – always busy round the house with her needle and thread. More so than me ..." When Andrew gave no answer, Elspeth continued "Of course, I know our Mary hasn't been the easiest person to live with. She always wanted her own way as a child. Dad always said she was the most selfish of the three of us."

Andrew looked at Elspeth, unhappy about what she might be about to say, but his look, although as distressed as he could make it, did nothing to dissuade Elspeth from her course.

"She likes to be the centre of attention, doesn't she – always busy doing something for someone. I expect, at times, that you felt you came pretty low down on the list, didn't you? You know, somewhere behind the Pilates group, the flower-arranging circle and the WI?"

It was a joke he himself had often made when the four of them sat round several bottles of wine and several wedges of cheese on a Friday night. Quite jokingly – for the sake of the conversation – he had suggested that he came forty-fifth in Mary's list of priorities. They all laughed – especially Mary, who commented that she didn't think "he was as far up the list as that" – accepting it to be the lot of most husbands. Somehow, at the time, it had seemed to take the tension out of any grievances that might have lain dormant in the conversation; now, coming from Elspeth, it didn't seem so funny and he was annoyed with his sister-in-law for deriding his wife.

"A friend of mine is a teaching assistant at the school. She tells me one or two things ... now and then. Mary can't do enough for her head, Sue, can she? It's surprising she hasn't got a deputy headship, yet."

"Mary enjoys her work – and yes, it's surprised me too," he replied, with the look that suggested Elspeth's skein of conversation had gone far enough.

"It'd be a crime to just let things fall apart," expostulated Elspeth, switching the discourse in a way he thought typical of women, and which he found most annoying.

"Elspeth ..."

When he paused, she urged him on with every gesture she knew – eyes full of expectation, hands open with understanding, mouth poised to offer advice.

"Yes?" she questioned, as he stalled.

"I'm not blaming Mary for what happened ..."

"Nevertheless ...?"

"No, I'm not – but what went wrong between us didn't just happen overnight. It takes a lifetime ... I don't see how we can even begin to unravel ..."

"Then don't – leave it alone. Live with it. We've had some good times together, and they'll be others in the future. If you persist in this, you'll not only lose Mary – you'll lose touch with all the family – yours and ours. Nothing will be the same again."

"Perhaps I don't want it to be."

"Oh for God's sake, Andy, grow up," she yelled, and looked about her to see who might have noticed; restraining herself, she said "If that's how you feel, there's nothing more to say. At least, I've tried. I just hope you realise what you're losing."

Did he? Andrew wasn't sure, as he drove home that evening. Away from it all and looking back, it didn't seem so bad. Perhaps he could have tried harder? His mind roved back over the reasons for the 'irretrievable breakdown' he'd given to the solicitor. 'Dad, those aren't reasons!' He heard Amy's voice, as clear as a bell.

But Mary had been dissatisfied with just about everything, and once the children no longer needed them there seemed little point in the struggle. It was clear that anyone who could complain as she did – from his not having "decorated the house for three years" to her "never having a dress to wear" could not be happy, or was determined (for whatever reason) *not* to be happy. That being the case, it seemed sensible to give her the chance to find someone who could give her what she needed – a handyman ever ready to wield the paintbrush or saw, the businessman who could whip her off on the requisite four holidays a year, the "normal" husband who would sit still and listen to her complaining about her job night after night, or most men who expected their wives to be snappy once a month every month forever …

Andrew pulled the car into a lay-by just before he reached the Orwell Bridge and sat still, taking deep breathes to stop himself from shaking. He knew he was being unfair. Lady mustn't see him like this: she'd be upset. She had been that time he collapsed in the garden.

'Dad, those aren't reasons!' Is that how Amy expected to behave towards her husband? Perhaps those villages he'd read about had the right idea. He couldn't think where they were now, but the women and men lived apart for most of the time. There was a 'women's house' where, presumably, they had nothing to moan about. The men went about their business, and the women theirs; the demarcation of labour seemed to work well. Everyone had someone to talk to – someone normal who would listen and could understand.

When he'd married, it'd been on the strength of programmes like *The Donna Reed Show* or, later, *The Dick van Dyke Show* with Mary Tyler Moore. They never seemed to argue – not abusively. It was shows and films like that and the books of his childhood that had formed his view of marriage. Men and women both knew their place, both understood their role: there was nothing to argue about. And there was always love, and he understood what that meant. Love wasn't so much about what you said (words are cheap and easy enough), but about how you behaved towards one another; it was that which required the effort and showed the sincerity of your feelings.

Chapter 21

A family wedding

It was Jonathan who, finally, made Andrew realise that the family had sided, in no uncertain terms, with Mary. She was the one, he explained, who had been "done to". The chance came – and Andrew felt that his son had seized the moment – at a family wedding.

Andrew had known about the wedding since the previous autumn but it had slipped his mind until Amy dropped by with her boyfriend and reminded him. "It's August 6th, dad," she said, "You haven't forgotten?" His smiled lie assured her he had, and she responded with a kiss on the cheek before dashing off to a music festival in the boyfriend's hired car.

The wedding was that of the son of Mary's older brother, Paul, who lived in the Midlands and who they saw only rarely. Amy told him that Mary was driving them all down to Newbury on the Friday, and that they would be "making a long weekend of it". Since the wedding was scheduled for 11 o'clock, Andrew decided that he, too, would have to stay over at least one night; he felt that longer might be both tedious and tense, since it would involve family get-togethers at which he didn't expect to be welcome.

The churchyard of St Mary's at Hamstead Marshall was criss-crossed by fluctuating bursts of shadow and sunshine; it was a typical August day, uncertain whether to bless the wedding or rain down upon it. Andrew wandered into the churchyard, alone, fifteen minutes or so before the service was due to start, expecting to find his family already seated and hoping to slide quietly onto the pew beside them.

Having a sentimental attachment to the Church of England, he'd always liked churchyards, and he stood for five minutes or so remembering his own wedding. That, also, had been in August on a bright sunny day in a country churchyard. He remembered vividly how Mary had worn a dress she'd made herself and how Elspeth had moaned at the bridesmaid's dresses – also homemade. Mary's veil had blown back in the breeze and framed her head like the hat of a lady at Ascot. The flowers, in peach and white to match the dresses, had tumbled in profusion from the hands of his sister and Elspeth. It had been rather formal, he recalled, with the traditional line-up of groups in the photographs and their respective mothers carrying handbags. The woman had all lost weight for the occasion and looked slender. Around her neck, Mary had worn the locket he gave her when they'd holidayed together, as students, in France. He'd spent hours cutting the two, minute photographs so that they fitted precisely into the heart-shaped frame. Smiles had been everywhere, and at the gate confetti showered over them. He remembered the smile she gave him as they left the church; the future had seemed rosy.

He hadn't made his promises lightly. He had meant what he said – "to have and to hold from this day forward, for better for worse, for richer for poorer, in sickness and in health, to love and to cherish, till death us do part ..." – at the time, and he knew that promises – 'troths', as the prayer book described them so elegantly – were binding. Oaths were not intended to be circumscribed by circumstances; yet, how could a man in his twenties – so young in the experience of the world – be expected to make such promises? How could anyone – man or woman – make such promises, and be held to keeping them? The experience of one's parents did not prepare anyone for marriage – whether their union had been happy or fraught with dissent was irrelevant. Each marriage was unique and had to seek its own fulfilment; each marriage was destined by forces outside the control of the couple. No – that he couldn't accept: each couple was responsible for their own success or failure – there was no passing the buck.

The sadness overwhelmed Andrew as he stood in the churchyard, recalling his own wedding day, and he thought he understood why so many women cried at weddings. They had a wisdom that was denied men – an understanding of what might be unless one was very careful, a feel for the fragility of relationships; that wisdom said a great deal about them.

The insight came and went in a moment; afterwards, he could recall it but never with the clarity of that instant. Thinking about it later, he wondered whether he had, simply, a sentimental view of women. He dismissed the notion; he had never been a cynic, and that day – his and Mary's day – had been filled with hope.

As Andrew entered the church, through the porch with the sunshine on his back, and was ushered down the aisle, it was Amy who saw him first. In a twinkling they all turned and looked at him and the expressions on their faces were ones that he knew he would take to the grave. Even in the horror of that second, he smiled at the cliché. Jonathan's expression could have been a sneer or maybe one of quiet contempt, Robert's one of bewilderment, Amy's of resignation mingled with sadness and Mary's one of disdain. He wasn't sure what each of them was saying, but the overall aspect was one of implacability; Andrew knew they were united against him. There were four of his family in the pew – five people altogether with the boyfriend – and there was room for him to join them should they decide to shuffle along, but they didn't: not one of them budged, and the look told him that they had no intention of doing so. He turned, quietly and with a deliberate intake of breath, and walked to the back of the church where he found a place among strangers.

He remembered little of the service: it was the proverbial blur to him. The words – from 'We have come together ...', when the bride and groom stood before the priest, to '... living together in faith and love ...' as he blessed them – swept over Andrew and oppressed him like a sickness. He was relieved to follow the happy couple out into the sunlight, and find a space for himself in the churchyard. Here, at least, he could breathe.

There was noise around him of many voices, shuffled movements and spasmodic laughter. The photographer called his name, and he was gripped by the arm and bundled into place in front of the white gates of the south facing porch for one family picture and then another. An old man passed him and asked permission to take "an informal shot for the bride's mother". "Look natural" he was told, and did so. '... there will be time to prepare a face to meet the faces that you meet': Eliot again.

He found himself a few feet away from Elspeth, who turned and smiled. He made towards her as a boat might make for the safety of a wharf, and became aware of Brian, his brother-in-law. Andrew stretched out his hand. Brian turned away, quite discreetly, ignoring the gesture. A group bustled by, between the gravestones. He hoped he didn't know them; he didn't want to speak – not just then. He had shared food, drink, holidays, conversation and laughter with this man who, now, didn't want to know him. Elspeth looked embarrassed and gave a smile that matched her husband's turn. "Nice day for a wedding," she offered, in a tone that would, in times past, have offered many meanings between the two of them, but was now no more than the pleasantry one might make to a stranger.

Somewhere, from across the churchyard, he caught the voices of his wife – ex-wife – and children. There was nothing to share now; he could make no easy stroll between these acquaintances to people who shared his sense of humour. Andrew found himself alone for, perhaps, the first time in his life; he had divorced more than a wife.

The photographer took the usual interminable time common to all wedding photographers but, eventually, Andrew saw groups gather and move towards the little, wooden gate, ready to wave off the newly-weds. The car was just outside ready for the short drive down the hill, and wedding guests lined the slope. Confetti was tossed and dropped in the hot air; there were smiles everywhere and hands waving. Andrew felt someone touch his arm. He didn't recognise the man at first, but then realized it was the father of Paul's wife. The old man was clearly embarrassed.

"I don't suppose you remember me?" he asked, by way of introduction.

"I must admit, I didn't at first – but, yes, you're Evelyn's father."

"Yes, that's right – Derek – Paul's wife's dad," insisted the old man, apparently determined to establish, firmly, the relationship.

"They've had a nice day for their wedding – your grandson and his wife."

"You never know how it's going to turn out, do you?" replied Derek. Andrew looked into the old eyes and smiled, sure that Derek had intended no double meaning in his remark. "I trust you're well," he continued, his eyes wet with age.

"Yes, thank you – and you?"

"As can be expected," murmured Derek, "Old age has few compensations. My wife and I do what we can to keep well. How is …?" His hesitation at saying "your family" or perhaps "your wife" did not alert Andrew to any underlying intention: he put it down to the old man's embarrassment at the idea of divorce. He remembered him as a kindly figure, and supposed he'd come out of a sense of courtesy. Andrew was grateful. "How are you? Are you well?" Derek continued.

"Teachers are always tired in August," replied Andrew, "I take about a month to recuperate once the term ends – but, yes thank you, on the whole I am well."

"I can imagine how tiring children must be, but you're lucky enough to be working at the right end of the market," Derek rejoined, and Andrew felt an unnecessary criticism was aimed at his profession in the lack of sympathy expressed.

"True," he responded, "but when I face over three hundred children each Monday morning in the school assembly, I do wonder how I cope, how my staff cope with their classes … and why so many public figures need notes when they speak."

The retaliation, couched though it was with a smile, was all the old man needed to pursue his mission. "It is felt," he whispered, "that your presence might add an unnecessary … and unwelcome air to the reception, and …" He paused, perhaps hoping that Andrew would complete the assignment for him, but Andrew was not given to easing social situations. If anyone had anything to say, let them have the courage to say it – and stand by their convictions. He hadn't seen the rejection coming, but now it had he was determined that the old man should justify his position.

"Are you telling me not to come?" he asked.

"Yes. It is felt that your being there would add tension to the proceedings … we hadn't expected you to attend the wedding," responded Derek, smiling as though the question was both stupid and unnecessary.

When Andrew persisted, by saying "Who has asked you to say this?" the old man shrugged, as though the matter was of no significance. Andrew insisted "I was invited."

"As a family, I am told."

The old man had out-manoeuvred him; to remain obdurate would make him look silly. Andrew glanced up, and realised they were being watched by a group that still hovered by the gate. Among them was Derek's wife, and Andrew drew his own conclusions as to who had ordered the assault on his dignity. When the old man returned to them, the look that his wife passed across the churchyard confirmed Andrew's suspicions.

Left alone in the churchyard, Andrew wandered across to the low wall that screened-off a section of the graveyard and gazed out across the gold and green of the Berkshire countryside. In the next field was what appeared to be a gatekeeper's lodge. Deckchairs lay toppled in the stubble and a table was being prepared for lunch.

Andrew looked about him, recalling Robert's invitation to his alternative birthday celebration – an occasion to which he supposed himself to be still looking forward. There was always the pub, of course. Where there's a church there's usually a pub; English villages are famous for the conjunction. Andrew smiled to himself. He still couldn't believe all this was happening; he could not accept that his family had actually turned their backs on him. Soon, he would wake up or come to his senses and return home. Once he did, would everything suddenly be all right? Would old Derek welcome him with a smile? Would family celebrations be open to him? Would Brian receive his outstretched hand? Would he and Mary sit with their in-laws once again, quaffing the Friday night bottle of wine?

Elspeth had reached out to him; he knew that, and realised she cared. Jack Tate had advised him in the only way he knew how. Amy had tried to reason with him and then cajole him. Robert had approached in that tentative way of his, saying little but meaning much. Elaine Price had warned him of the consequences of his actions, sitting in the Buttermarket drinking coffee. Now the decree had become absolute, had their attitudes changed?

He could not accept the feelings of hostility towards him. He had faced the anger of parents without batting an eyelid; he had accepted their right to be upset at times if they were concerned about their children. He had always been able to absorb and dissipate their anger; he had been the agent of conciliation. This hostility was quite different. His family, friends and relations knew him as a loving family man; surely they could see that he hadn't acted lightly, or without thought? Surely they could see that he had reasons. '... Dad, those aren't reasons!' Amy's words returned.

"Dad?" called a voice he recognised as Jonathan's, and he turned to see his son approaching from the church gate. "Mum thought I ought to see if you were OK? We heard what Evelyn's father had said."

"Won't you miss the reception," Andrew responded, inanely, not bothering to wonder how news of the old man's intervention had reached their ears.

"They're busy with more photographs. No one's eating yet."

"That's OK, then."

They both laughed at the shared humour – the implication (not to be taken at face value) that Jonathan would not have come if the meal had started – and walked over to the shelter of the churchyard wall where they sat, for a while, in silence. Andrew had no desire to speak; all he wanted was to curl up into a ball, somewhere, and sleep. He was so exhausted, but knew he had to hear what his son had to say.

"We can't reconcile what we have been to each other in the past with what is happening now," Jonathan explained, eventually.

"The past cannot be changed, Jonathan. What I was then, I was – you cannot alter that to fit in with this new view of me. I was a good father to all of you. You have to reconcile that with what I have now done – and accept that I acted in good faith."

"But that's what we can't do – and, please, let me finish. This is difficult enough without you interrupting my train of thought."

"Sorry," replied Andrew.

"We all lived happily as a family and now this has happened. We can't seem to build bridges to the future – not without you there in the family home. We can understand your adultery. It's very common with men of your age – no, don't interrupt, or I'm going – but we can't understand why you've rushed ahead so quickly with the divorce. Mum pleaded with you to just live separately for however long you wanted – and let me say we thought that was big of her, considering what had happened – but you wouldn't have it, would you? You couldn't wait to gain your freedom – as you call it. We can't reconcile the tenderness we all shared together with the ruthless way you have acted.

You've left mum in a terrible position – she feels alone, disgraced, humiliated. She goes about like a zombie. She can't believe what has happened, and we have to live with that – day in, day out. She does everything she can to remain calm and collected. She carried on at work until the end of term, she attends her WI and flower-arranging and Pilates ... and whatever, trying to make it seem as though things will come right in the end. But she's going to crack – we all know that and dread it. She sits for hours – when she's not going on about whatever-her-name-is – crying. She feels that, in some way, it's her fault – which, clearly, it isn't – and that people despise her. You can't imagine how difficult it was getting her to come to this wedding.

She's wounded, dad, and it's only you who can put that right. We can be there for her, but it's you she wants. She can't conceal the hurt she feels ... and she's terrified of being left alone in her old age. There's no one she can really turn to – not once we've gone, and mum knows we won't be there forever. We've got our own lives to lead. You're the only person she's ever been able to confide in – the only one she's ever been able to open up her soul to – and now, you've gone. You're the only one who she's ever been able to share her true feelings with – you know that, don't you?

Come back – now – to the reception. We'll stand by you. There's no way we'd allow you to be treated like this – dismissed by virtual strangers. All you have to do is give mum a chance to ... state her case ... later."

Although they were close as a family, the closeness was tacit. They were not people who shared their feelings so openly as Jonathan had just done; any such show of emotion was more likely to have been buried in humour. It was a rare moment for the two of them, but Andrew knew that to return as his son wished would be both dishonest and – more importantly to him at that stage – unworkable. His son, in desperation, was attempting to effect a reconciliation that, if it came at all, would have to be in its own time.

Chapter 22

Brief encounter

In the days that followed his children's involvement in his dismissal from yet another family celebration, Andrew's loneliness closed in. Even Lady's "little ways" that normally brought him – and previously the family – so much amusement did nothing to distract him. Smelling his coffee brewing, she would peer doe-eyed round the door for her "coffee time treat", nudge him when it was time for that final evening walk or drop her soft toys at his feet when she wanted company, but Andrew remained impervious to her charms. While the Cocker spaniel crouched in the corner of the small sitting room of the cottage, watching him with bewildered eyes, Andrew came to realise that he was losing his sense of humour, and the knowledge left him terrified.

His mind roved back over what his son, Jonathan, had said in the churchyard, and he refused to make any sense of it. They had "lived happily as a family", and perhaps that was part of the problem: he had made marriage look too easy.

He could understand their inability to "build bridges to the future". They felt bereaved; it was as though a key member of the family had died, and they could see no way ahead without them. Death always brought shock and, often, rage at the unfairness of it all. Andrew had felt the same when his mother died so young: she had only been in her sixties, and her loss had left him desolated. He could see that it was the same for his family, now.

He couldn't tell them why he had "rushed ahead" as he did; he couldn't tell them that without going into the interminable and tortuous conversations he'd had with Mary over the years. These had gone round and round in circles, on and on through long, whispered evenings after the children were asleep. They had come to an understanding about each other's feelings and needs, and they had 'made up': but it had made no difference to their behaviour. The next time their feelings, needs, views ... whatever, diverged there had always been the inevitable altercation. Some men, he had been told, relished that; he never had, and he abhorred, each time, the verbal slagging-off he received. How could he talk to his children about that without betraying Mary?

He knew Mary was "in a terrible position" – what other people thought had always been a central consideration for her – but what could he do, if going back was not an option?

He could sympathise with his children having to "live with it". Oh, yes, he could sympathise with their predicament! Again, what could he do but return and try – with an increasing sense of futility – to put things right. "She's wounded, dad, and it's only you who can put that right". Andrew knew it was true; he also knew it was what those wedding vows had been about so many years ago.

He was the only person she'd ever been able to confide in – the only one she'd ever been able to open up her soul to – and now, he was gone. He'd failed to make her happy, and now he'd given up trying. 'An in-built dissatisfaction': that was the phrase he'd used with the solicitor. "Yes," she'd said, "I can do something with that." Without actually saying anything, he'd wished her luck. He'd never been able to come up to scratch.

Andrew looked at Lady, and could see she was frightened. It was strange and wonderful how dogs surmised and shared your feelings. He felt sorry for her, crouched as she was in the corner, and reached out to fondle her ears.

"Come on, Lady," he said, "let's go for a walk. Let's try and walk these blues away."

They crossed the road from their new 'home' and took the signposted walk that led them round the churchyard. The now familiar smells drew Lady in, but Andrew felt no joy in her excitement. She was just another dog running around. Normally, he would have laughed as she spooked a rabbit, chased a butterfly or snuffled the side of the track for dropped crumbs, but not today. He had never lost his sense of humour before; dark it may have been, but it was always present – until now. 'Now' was the time he had broken faith with his promises and betrayed those he loved, and who depended upon him. He couldn't see himself coming to terms with that; it was something he would have to live with – forever.

When the children had been growing up, life had never seemed better. They both had professional jobs they enjoyed and which supported their lives, but the work hadn't been the 'be all and end all'. Getting home had been the main obsession – getting home to be with the family.

They shared so many interests and had a similar outlook: they talked, they read, they discussed literature and politics and religion ... you had but to name it! Mary had been an individual – someone who thought things out for herself, and didn't just snap up the latest point of view from the media. She could think, and their intellects rubbed off on their three children. Andrew had always been proud of the fact that their children could think for themselves, and would never run with the mob. "If everybody thinks it," he had once said, "you can be pretty sure of one thing – it's wrong!" They'd all laughed in agreement.

She'd had her own interests too – those Jonathan had listed, and more. She made a life for herself, while he was content to stay at home of an evening and be with the children. It had been an easy life, which had flowered as the children got older and developed their own interests and activities. All three played an instrument and were involved in musical ensembles; all three excelled at one sport or another. Time was absorbed in these pursuits.

They'd been lucky, of course: their both being teachers meant that all holidays and high days were shared with the children. As a family, they spent huge amounts of time together. It was something none of them thought about: it was, quite simply, taken for granted.

In those days, he'd never asked himself how Mary saw her place in the family. She was his wife and the children's mother; his intellect never took him further than acceptance of the fact. Yet he had been aware, even then, of the web that was being spun around him. He hadn't resented it: the strands held the family together, and he was grateful. Within him, however, there grew a sense of wanting to be free – not of his wife or his children, but of being entrapped. There had always been a 'scene' – however trivial at times – whenever his interests had cut across Mary's or the children's. If he was committed to going somewhere that conflicted with their needs, it was his activities which had to be re-arranged.

Moreover, he had become very successful at his job; the school of which he was headteacher was well-known for its innovations. The more this was acknowledged within the education authority, the more it seemed to irritate Mary, and encouraged snappish comments whenever he spoke of the work of his staff. He put this down to jealousy, and then dismissed the idea as silly. Mary could no more be envious of his success than he would have been of her achievements.

Whenever he had a commitment which took over a weekend or involved him being away from home for more than an evening, Andrew always prepared himself for a confrontation; this took much of the joy from his endeavours. Sometimes – even if the children and she were not directly inconvenienced – Mary would assume a cold demeanour towards him, remaining strangely aloof to his activities, and seeming to hold them in the light of a quiet disdain. At other times, Mary seemed almost to welcome them, but as though they were something of no consequence – games for the boys. Andrew didn't like this; he felt that she should, at least, share his enthusiasm.

At such times he feared her, seeing her attitudes as a threat to his independence.

It was in the middle of August that the phone rang one morning as he returned from his first walk with

Madge; he was getting used to the sound. Amy was in France, waiting for the grape-picking, Robert was in Spain at the beginning of his year abroad and Jonathan had started a belated gap year by travelling to Thailand to lie on the beach. Mary phoned him every day, and Andrew got used to ignoring the ring and checking with the voicemail. When he did on this morning, it was Elaine Price's voice he heard, asking him if he would ring her when it was convenient.

He picked up the phone and called back immediately. Elaine was clearly very agitated about something and wanted to see him as soon as possible. Could they meet somewhere for lunch, one day, he asked. He heard the hesitation, followed by the reluctant agreement, with some degree of perplexity, but assumed the anniversary of Julian's suicide, which was fast approaching, to be the reason.

He looked forward, with more pleasure than he cared to admit, to meeting with Elaine. She struck him as a woman who had coped in extreme circumstances – someone with real problems who had pulled herself through them by sheer independence.

He had suggested the Oyster Reach, which would avoid the heat of the town, and met her there two days later. She was wearing a long, flowing white dress, and looked cool and fresh in the summer heat; it took his breathe away. He noticed, for the first time, that her hair was dark – dark as the wing of a bird, he thought. Andrew recalled her having grey flecks, and supposed he must have been wrong. Perhaps it was the occasion he remembered, fraught with Julian's death?

"Hello," he said, "no children today?"

"My mother's looking after them – for the day, in fact. Enjoying the holidays?"

"So, so: now the children are older, holidays don't have the same attraction."

"Oh, I love them: can't wait for them to come round."

"Have you been away?"

"No – no money for that, but Rosie and Matt have had a good time. We've been out nearly every day, and my parents are very good. I suppose you heads are busy planning for next term?"

"No, I got all that ready before we broke up."

"Really?"

"Yes," he replied, feeling as unreal as the occasion. He hadn't expected her to bring the children – so why had he pretended otherwise? She hadn't expected him to be enjoying the holidays, either – not knowing that he was going through a divorce – and Andrew wondered why they were skirting whatever issue had brought them together.

"Shall we … eh, go through?"

Elaine smiled – relieved, it seemed, that things were moving forward. The pub had been modernised and served a variety of real ales. The menu offered the usual range of food expected in pubs nowadays; Andrew thought they might be better off specialising in a smaller amount of genuinely home-cooked food, and chose one of the day's specialities, hoping this would fit the bill.

As they waited for the meal to arrive – Andrew with his pint of Old Hooky and Elaine with a small, dry white wine – it was Elaine who broke the stalemate.

"Where you aware," she asked, "that we are considered to be an 'item'?"

"I gathered that I was ... associated with someone, but I didn't know ... I wasn't sure who it was," he answered, not wanting to enter into a discussion regarding his children's suppositions.

"A friend told me as soon as we broke up. I've been stewing on it ever since, and I couldn't go back to school with this hanging over me."

"No, of course not," Andrew replied, desperate to sound reasonable. "You've no idea where the gossip came from?"

"It doesn't matter, does it? It's a question of what we do about it. I take it that you do want to do something about it?"

"We can't *do* anything," Andrew replied.

"You think it will make matters worse?"

"Yes – any denial will simply make people believe it more."

"You seem very calm about it, Andrew?"

"It doesn't appeal to me, if that's what you mean. I wouldn't have chosen for this to happen simply to flatter my male ego, but it has happened – and we are helpless."

"But it's untrue. I don't want to be looked on as 'the other woman'."

"There is no other woman," he insisted with an edge to his voice, which Elaine did not fail to notice. "I expect someone saw us having coffee in town – it's as simple as that, but any explanations we offer will simply sound like excuses ... Do you want to leave – we might be seen here, and that would compound the damage."

"No ... yes ... I don't see why we should. We're doing nothing wrong."

"If anyone sees us, it will be assumed that we booked in here and that this is the precursor to an afternoon of lustful couplings."

"It's all very well to joke," she laughed, "but women can be very bitchy. If it was thought that I'd broken up your marriage, it would be very unpleasant when I return to work in a couple of weeks' time."

"Yes, I can see that, but we can only strike the royal pose – never apologise, never explain."

"You really think that to do so will make matters worse?"

The meals arrived and Andrew tucked into his chicken breast wrapped in bacon, while Elaine picked at hers, pushing the paprika chicken salad around the plate and sipping her wine.

"People know my situation – or think they do. It will be supposed that I see you as a good catch. A single mother with two children to bring up must be looking for a husband."

Andrew thought that to be only a woman's way of looking at the world, but said nothing.

"It's assumed that us single mothers are always on the lookout for a likely man. No one – none of our married friends, that is – asks themselves why we should be ready to make the same mistake again ... Once betrayed you do tend to look at things differently ... not that I'm suggesting ..." She paused, waiting for Andrew to reassure her, but he remained silent. "I don't want to ... appear imprudent. I have a reputation for being headstrong ..."

"Is that what brought you and Julian together?"

"Yes – what made you say that?" she asked and, when Andrew shrugged, continued "Mary told you?"

"Gossip."

"But you see what I mean? We need to understand each other otherwise we're going to find ourselves in a situation not of our making ..."

Andrew thought of Jack Tate and his inopportune advice, but could not imagine himself being propelled along by the assumptions of others and said so.

"You might be able to ignore it, Andrew, but I can't. It's different for women. Look how highly Julian was regarded, and yet it was him who left me. People aren't always very fair in their opinions. They don't always understand, and are quick to criticise. I have many colleagues at work, but I'm not sure that I have one friend I could rely on. I've had enough ups and downs over the past three years to last me a lifetime."

"Very well – if it's mentioned to me, I will deny it, but the denial will do no good, and is more than likely to do harm."

"Thank you ... you're right, there's no need to raise it as an issue, but if you do hear a whisper, I'd be grateful if you'd do all you could to refute it ... I know we are both free people, but ..." Elaine shrugged, as though the movement was significant.

"Another drink?" he asked.

"No, thank you," she replied, and then, as he rose, continued "Are you having one? Then I will."

It struck him, as he walked to the bar, that Elaine was rather enjoying the lunch. When he returned with the drinks, she surprised him by saying so.

"It's the chance to talk with another adult," she explained, "I spend all my time conversing with children."

"So, despite the fact that you'd think twice before getting involved with anyone again, you do miss male company?"

"I missed Julian. I missed his humour and his unreasonableness," she laughed. "My friends urged me to find someone else, but I told them it was useless."

"Anyone else would be second best?"

"Julian and I had two children together ... and it makes a difference."

Andrew could see what Elaine was saying and realised he'd hit some nail or other on the head, but he didn't agree with her reservations. Each relationship, he thought, must have its own uniqueness; comparing one with the other would be both pointless and offensive. He wondered, as he watched her eating more eagerly now that he had agreed to scotch any rumours, why he was thinking like this at all. Nothing had been further from his mind when he'd suggested lunch in response to her phone call.

"I found it difficult living on my own at first, but you get used to it, and I rather think I'd resent giving up my independence now. How are you coping?"

"Well – men of my age aren't as inept at running the home as women like to think. After all, we are the first generation to be married to working wives. We've had to cope."

They talked on into the afternoon. Elaine relived her husband's suicide once again and, Andrew felt, unburdened herself as one never can in talking with children. When they looked up, the pub had emptied of other lunchtime customers, and they were both aware that they had enjoyed each other's company. He walked Elaine to her car, said goodbye and wished he had walked along the Strand rather than driven by road: somehow, she had given him a lot to think about.

CHAPTER 23

The railway station

It was Sunday evening, and Andrew had driven out to the railway station at Westerfield where, for Julian, all predicaments had been resolved and where, for Andrew, his current plight seemed to have begun.

He'd arrived home from his meeting with Elaine to find yet another of Mary's letters waiting for him. Sometimes, he would leave them unopened but place them carefully in the drawer of his desk. His desk – huh, at least he had a kitchen table to work on in the rented cottage, but not his desk. That was at home in the study surrounded by his books and his thoughts from over the many years he and Mary had been together.

This time, Andrew had opened the letter and read it. He couldn't explain why: perhaps it was his feelings of guilt at having enjoyed his time with Elaine? Such pleasures must be paid for – each joy tempered with a matching sadness. Mary's letter took the same tone as those he had troubled himself to read; it was conciliatory, urging him to return home where they could be together.

Dear Andy,

You sounded so sad when we spoke on the phone, and so wretched in thinking that the children don't love you and want you anymore. It's not true. They love you dearly and miss your friendship deeply. It would be silly of me to say that there wouldn't be bridges to build – of course there would, but when you love and cherish someone – and they do – then nothing is impossible. They're disturbed by events and they want to be close to you again as part of the loving and caring family we built for them – the kind of family that can live and enjoy life together. That's what they're saying to me. At heart you're a decent and loving person. They know that – believe me, love – but it's us that must lead the way, if we could be more sharing of a life together. You know I'd give anything to be your wife again.

Our children need to see us as a source of love, support and pleasure in their lives. They need the security of the love and comfort of a good home together. I truly hate us not being together so that we can look forward to – one day – being grandparents and watching our grandchildren grow and flourish together in happiness – our happiness as well as theirs.

I love you, Andy. Let's try and move forward in shared love and family life. Come into our lives again. We miss you so much. Life is too short for lasting rifts. Let's try and find some peace. Surely, at our age, we should have enough wisdom to find a way?

Take care,
Mary

He could see her writing it – the tears flowing down her cheeks. How many times in the past had he wiped those dry, only to have them flow again at the next emotional crisis?

He'd folded the letter carefully, slid it back into the envelope and laid it with the others. He'd then tickled Madge between the ears and taken her for a walk, saying "Come on, Lady. Let's find some fresh air."

Andrew's thoughts of his disloyalty to his family were mingled with those of an awakening interest in Elaine Price – something of which he had not been conscious before their lunch together. Thinking about her, he remembered that each time – and there had been only a few times – he met Elaine, Andrew had found her 'fresh and new'. Although the phrase made no sense, he couldn't express it in any other way; it explained nothing to him. It was just that – an expression of feeling.

Had she sat in silence, Elaine would have intrigued him. Moreover, he had – if he were honest – found himself, when he was away from her, wondering about what she had been doing, thinking about how she was coping.

The brief moments they'd spent together – standing by her car after the news of Julian's suicide had become gossip, sharing a coffee in the Buttermarket or lunching at the Oyster Reach – had been important to him.

He knew little of her, but thought her to be needy. Yet, he realised that this was only his perception and that the need might be his: after all, in the next thought, he saw her as vigorously independent and well able to cope.

Whenever they were close, he had been overwhelmed by her presence. Their very proximity had conveyed an intimacy that was implied rather than acknowledged. When their eyes met, they had both smiled, even though Elaine was not one to whom smiling came naturally, he felt. Standing by her car – nearly a year ago now – he had

220

wanted to take her in his arms, hold her close and take away the pain.

He struggled with the acceptance of this knowledge, and recognised that he liked Elaine Price. 'Like' was a word he'd come to struggle with over the years. He had known 'love' and appreciated that 'love' was important; he did not share the cynical view of 'love' as a tool with which we are manipulated. He wondered, however, whether enough significance was attached to 'like'. While 'love' was inclined to be a nebulous mix of feelings, we always knew what we 'liked' about people. What he liked about Elaine Price was her independent spirit, her quiet smile in the face of unimaginable pain, her unflagging care for her children, her optimism in the face of reality, her company, her sense of proportion ... Andrew wondered what he didn't like about her, and then why these particular likeable qualities were the ones that drew his attention.

Oh, and he liked her quiet voice. Walking Madge on the day they'd enjoyed lunch together – and for the days that followed his acceptance of these feelings – Andrew recalled Elaine's quiet voice. There was a naturalness about her tone that he found attractive; her voice was free from hysteria. She faced life honestly and, when she was not sad, there was a smile in her words. Somewhere in this woman there were experiences of life which he had barely glimpsed; she was beyond the shallowness of others.

Allowing himself to think like this, Andrew perceived that he should not have met her as he had done; he began to define a dishonesty in his motives that, he accepted, may or may not have been real. He didn't want an affair with her – nothing was further from his mind: of that he was sure. He also knew that he could not speak to her of his feelings or his thoughts, while acknowledging that he wanted to spend time with her; he believed that he could sit beside her, quite still, forever.

He had a vision of them together, and he shook it from him like the raindrops of a summer shower.

On the platform, he waited for the six o'clock train. In coming here, Andrew was aware that he was close to his family. On the night he had learned of Julian's suicide, it was to this station that he had walked with Madge. He was conscious of a hope – a silly and vague hope – that, somehow, his family would know he was here and would come to him. As he waited on the bench, Andrew even rehearsed the conversation he would hold with whichever one of his children should come walking along the platform.

He could see why Julian had chosen death; it must have seemed the only way out of an impossible and dishonourable situation. How much had he suffered during those two years he was away from his family? Respected by so many in his work, while – at the same time – knowing he had betrayed his wife and children, the man must have seen nowhere to turn; it was the dichotomy that had destroyed him – the inability to reconcile the differences within the same person.

Andrew looked along the track, and he realised how simple it was – once the decision had been made – to end the contradictions and the heartache. He was conscious of the anger within him – an anger that was due to the resentments he had allowed to gather over the years. Far, far better to have had it out – to have entered into a catalogue of rows – than to be sitting alone on a railway station waiting for the train.

The shadows of his anger passed over him, and he was surrounded by the darkness of rage. Death held no fears for him at that moment; death would be a merciful release ... and a punishment for those who had wronged him. How would they feel once he had gone – he who was not permitted to be free and without whom they would all collapse in ruins? Would they miss him? Would they be able to continue their lives – lives that now seemed only possible at the expense of his freedom?

Andrew noticed his hands trembling and, despite the warmth of the August evening, he shivered. He needed to explain; if only someone, to whom he could explain, would come. He was not a bad person; he was a 'decent and loving' man. Why had no one acknowledged that during the years he had devoted to his family? He apprehended the life blood being sucked from him, remorselessly and without compunction.

He remembered the many times he had left his bed during the night, fearing for one child or the other, and his relief when he found them sleeping safely and soundly. He had loved them at such times; he had loved them deeply and with an overwhelming tenderness.

Then, he thought of the quarrels with Mary that he could not bear and how they had stuck like shafts in his sides and chest. He had yearned for a soft voice and a gentle nature, and wondered whether that was too much to ask from life; he had wondered whether anyone deserved that, and why some men appeared to achieve it so effortlessly. He was not made for this world; he had done his bit, as well as he could, and was ready for the next. Somewhere there was a place where tranquillity was the order of the day, where hope was not sullied by despair and where thoughts could remain unspoken. He couldn't explain the mysteries of the world or solve its problems. He didn't want to – not any more. As a young man, he had felt differently: the world had been opened to him, and he relished its challenge.

He saw the train approaching, slowly and with a laborious trundle of the heavy iron wheels. It clattered by with that peculiar and comforting rhythmic sound as it passed over the joins in the rails, and then was gone. Andrew looked at his watch: it was later than he'd thought and Madge would be waiting for her walk.

CHAPTER 24

The Lakes

The autumn term passed quickly and was, as always, full of activity for staff and children. Parents' evenings were followed by the Harvest Festival – to which every class contributed an item of poetry, song, dance, music or drama – and the term ended on that perennial high note – Christmas. Andrew, absorbed in his work, enjoyed it; there was little time to think about your personal life when you worked with over three hundred children every day. The Early Years children were performing *The Snow Queen*, and he had been commandeered to see to the lighting effects; he was in his element. Work excluded everything else, while it absorbed him.

Jonathan had returned from Thailand and taken a lucrative job with an IT company, Robert wrote regularly about how much he was enjoying his time at the university in Barcelona where he was pursuing his Spanish studies and Amy – minus the boyfriend of the summer – was "having a blast" at Essex University with a group of girlfriends. Only Robert wrote frequently – on the basis of one letter a week that he sent, alternately, to his mother or father. It was from Mary's phone calls that Andrew gathered most of the information about his children.

These came with increasing frequency as the term progressed, and with varying degrees of virulence and amiability. Time and again, Mary tried to coax or coerce him into meeting her – a Sunday lunch, a trip to see their daughter, a holiday excursion – and each time he refused.

Occasionally, he met Elaine Price in town. There was a casual bond between them by now – brought on by their solicitousness towards each other; the bitchiness she had feared during the summer had not materialised. It became a ritual – spasmodic and always tempered with a feigned surprise – that they met for coffee on a Saturday morning while her children were in drama classes. Inevitably, as the term progressed, Christmas became a pervasive topic of conversation – at first, in connection with work and then with their own celebrations.

Christmas had been a sore point between Mary and himself from early on in the term when she had re-iterated her comment "If you persist in this, you'll never spend another Christmas with your children ... I shall see that you don't." He didn't share this ultimatum with Elaine – they rarely talked directly about their divorces – but, by November, Andrew had accepted the truth of those few words: their chill haunted him, and Elaine picked up on his anxiety.

"You mean you're going to spend Christmas alone?" she asked, and his plight didn't sound so bad; coming from another's lips it almost carried a sense of relief.

"I think that looks likely, at the moment."

"You can't keep running away, Andrew. The longer you leave it, the more difficult it will be to take the bull by the horns."

"I don't understand," he lied – amazed, as always, at the perceptiveness of women – and listened while she explained.

"I can't seem to do that," he replied when Elaine had finished, "It would put my children in a difficult position."

"They have a choice to make, Andrew, and you're not giving them the chance. Ask them – they might be only too willing to come to you for Boxing Day."

But if they felt they shouldn't, and refused him? Andrew didn't feel he could face that kind of rejection. He understood how they might be pressured into ignoring him at a wedding or arranging a separate birthday party, but could he bear a direct refusal to visit? He didn't think so, and was unwilling to put the issue to the test.

"How are you spending your Christmas?" he asked, without interest, only wishing to turn the conversation from himself.

"We're having my parents round on the big day. The children like to be at home, and so I told my mother straight that I was putting on Christmas this year. She likes to organise ... Ask your children, Andrew."

"You think I'm being cowardly?"

"I can understand why you hesitate ... but, yes! They have as much need to see you as you do to see them."

"You think so?"

"I know so. You tell me that Robert writes every week."

"Yes – he's a good correspondent."

"Then correspond with him. I don't mean in letters – I expect you do that – I mean by talking to him. He'll be home for Christmas soon, won't he?"

"Yes – he is coming, although we didn't expect him. We thought he might want to stay in Spain for the occasion."

"You mustn't let unhappiness take you over, Andrew. Your family wouldn't want that for you."

"I don't mind being alone, and I wouldn't want to cause any kind of conflict within the family."

"There is conflict, Andrew – you're divorced, and Mary isn't going to forgive you. Your children need to know your point of view."

"I don't think so …"

"I know so."

"… and, anyway, it isn't something I'd want to discuss in detail with them. It's between Mary and me."

"Not any longer. You're running away, Andrew. Your children love you – embrace them."

The following day – it was Sunday and Andrew was preparing his assembly for the next morning – the phone rang. He ignored it, fearing a long conversation with Mary, but checked the voicemail soon after the ringing had ceased. It was Elaine Price, asking him to call back. He did.

"I couldn't say this, yesterday," she said, "not to your face … Don't ask me why … If you won't ask your children round, and are going to be alone, would you like to share Boxing Day with us? I can't ask you for the Christmas Day because my mother would begin endless speculations, but Boxing Day would be OK. Don't misinterpret what I'm saying, Andrew. I'm asking you round for a meal – that's all. You shouldn't be alone all Christmas."

Elaine's intentions were not clear to Andrew. She had been nothing but kind to him; he had no right to make assumptions, but could not shake off a shiver of excitement at her invitation. He could not believe that a woman would make such a suggestion without having what would be called 'an ulterior motive', and was angry with the cheapness of his thinking. It was a thought that belittled the woman, and showed that he did not altogether trust his own motives. Her talk, during the summer, of them being 'an item' could not – surely – have been a blind, could it? She had certainly shown no reluctance to join him for coffee when the term re-started.

But no – he did not believe his own surmises. They were merely the natural musings of a man – a free man – for an attractive woman, and Elaine Price was an attractive woman. The conjectures were his – not hers – and he had been flattered by nothing but his own vanity. He recalled Elaine's voice and face as they had talked; her whole manner had been open, and her concerns had been only for him.

Why should Elaine – after her terrible experience of marriage – be remotely interested in an ageing schoolteacher who was a failure in his private life? What could he possibly have to offer anyone, let alone a woman struggling to bring up two young children? She would have enough on her hands, without having to introduce her children to someone they would only see as an intruder.

Andrew realised that he had little or nothing to offer anyone; he had no life outside his own family. Apart from his working life, he had no existence.

To even think of beginning another life with someone else would involve him in … in what – in learning another language – a language that Elaine Price must have had to learn long ago – the language of the dispossessed? He was entering a world that he did not understand because he had never lived there. He had never lived anywhere that was not recognisably 'home'.

This world had been Elaine's for several years; it was a world she understood – hence her advice to seek out his children before it was too late, before the schism that was opening up between then grew any wider. He felt this longing to talk with her again, seeing her as someone who might open his eyes; yet it was a road down which he had no desire to travel.

The following weekend, when they met for coffee and he politely declined Elaine's offer, did he detect a chill in her voice or was it with relief that she heard his refusal?

Andrew had made his decision rapidly and intuitively. He would spend Christmas alone in a place he had always loved – the Lake District: this would save his children any embarrassment. When he told Elaine – mainly, as he thought, to put her mind at rest over his well-being – she smiled but said nothing.

The cottage he rented was in the village of Grasmere. Madge explored the garden, while he settled in. 'Settling in' was a major preoccupation with Andrew. At home, he had always been the one to draw the curtains against a winter night and turn on the lamps, to rush ahead when they arrived home from a holiday to make his children's bedrooms cosy, to tidy away and put everything in its place after any festivities; he needed to restore order to even the smallest chaos.

He unpacked, hanging his shirts and trousers, placing his boots and shoes in the bottom of the wardrobe, putting the heavy wax coat on the back door hook with the dog's lead, placing shaving gear and toothbrush in the bathroom, laying his pants and socks in a drawer, arranging the books he intended to read beside the bed, sorting the maps and guidebooks onto the sitting room table and the food he had brought onto the long table in the kitchen. He then called Madge, fed her and poured himself a beer.

The promised log fire had been laid and he soon had the flames roaring up the chimney. He settled back into the armchair and looked around. It was all he could have wished – stone or wooden floors with the occasional rug, heavy winter curtains that he closed against the late afternoon, plain beams studded with odd hooks and nails, wooden furniture polished with beeswax.

He reached into a casual bag he'd hung from the back of one of the chairs at the table, pulled out a packet of small cigars and drew in the smoke. No one said anything and he pretended this surprised him; he smiled, wishing only that his oldest son who also enjoyed a smoke at Christmas was sitting opposite with a tumbler of whisky in his hand. Madge settled at his feet, basking in the glow of the fire.

It was December 23rd; all hell would be loose at home as the family dashed about heeding Mary's needs and helping her catch up with herself, but he was no longer caught in the middle of it. It was to be a lonely Christmas but a quiet one – the most enjoyable he had known since the pleasure of the children when they were small. Robert, the quiet one, would bring stillness to the occasion, but Jonathan would be off as soon as he could with the girl he'd met at the office and Amy wouldn't be able to wait to go clubbing with her friends.

He thought of the meal he wouldn't share and the games he wouldn't play, and Andrew regretted being alone. It was Robert who caught his attention because he was the one who drew most from family get-togethers. Andrew regretted his isolation as he thought of Robert, and realised the selfishness of what he had done. He was Robert's father, after all: it wasn't right to leave him alone – especially at Christmas.

Andrew looked at Madge and rubbed her ears. He thought they'd take a walk before the light went altogether. Madge might enjoy an excursion round the lake at least as far as the footbridge where Grasmere flowed into Rydal Water. Their cottage was just on the edge of the village, but they wouldn't go there this afternoon. He'd brought something to cook for supper; tomorrow would be soon enough to seek out their Christmas fare.

The next morning, Andrew sauntered into the village of Grasmere with Madge at his side. He had already planned the Christmas Day meal, and the shopping took him no time at all. Having enjoyed a coffee at the Miller Howe Cafe and lugged the bags home to their cottage, he was free to set out on his favourite trail – a short walk they would take at a leisurely pace, enjoying lunch and a drink at the Badger Bar before returning home along the banks of Rydal Water. It was known in the guide books as the Wordsworth Walk; it began, for Andrew, at Dove Cottage and reached Rydal Mount – the poet's final home – at the half-way point.

It was a steep climb from Dove Cottage – steeper than he had remembered – but the hard road soon gave way to a terraced walk. On his left was a bracken-covered slope and, looking down to his right, Andrew could see Rydal Water beyond the line of trees.

Wordsworth's poetry had a profound influence on Andrew as a young man; it was an influence that had never left him. In the poem known as *Lines written a few miles above Tintern Abbey*, Wordsworth expressed the belief that our natural surroundings had a profound influence on our view of the world – on 'our little, nameless, unremembered acts of kindness and of love'. He ascribed to nature the power to 'lift the burden of the mystery' and create 'that serene and blessed mood, in which ... with an eye made quiet by the power of harmony, and the deep power of joy, we see into the life of things'.

He had struggled to find that mood in marriage and, at times, it had been there for him and, he hoped, his family; but all too often the will had replaced the reflective mood and the struggle for dominance had driven out the serenity. The world drove in upon you and closed you down, whereas it should have led you on to wisdom. Somehow, however, he couldn't let it go and descend into the cynicism and trite philosophy adopted by the old to excuse their failures. He had felt 'a presence' and been disturbed 'with the joy of elevated thoughts'; he knew what Wordsworth meant by 'a sense sublime of something far more deeply interfused'.

If it was to nurture this sense, marriage – for that was the landscape in which we lived – was about those 'little, nameless, unremembered acts of kindness and of love'. Love was shown in the way you spoke each to the other, it rolled through all aspects of your life together; it did not choose its moments to be nice, it did not select its sentiments from the words on valentine cards and it left no room for rancour. Love was about what you did, not what you said; in love, there was no room for din.

Thinking these thoughts as he walked, Andrew realised why he had left and felt some confidence in the future begin to surge through his heart. He had taken the irrevocable step – regardless, it is true, of his family's feelings, but he had spent his life regarding theirs and now his family, if they chose to do so, must regard his – and there could be no turning back. To do that would negate everything that he – in his darkest moments – had felt and resolved, once he was free, to reconcile.

It was a hard task he was undertaking, but Andrew felt that he must see it through, and trust to a happy ending. He realised, now, that he could not – as he had always felt obliged to do – take the overall blame for their conflicts along the way. He had never before applied Wordsworth's view of the natural landscape to the landscape of his life; he had simply held on to the idea that somewhere, amid the din, there had been a place or a time where harmony might be found. He realised, too, that no one else could lead him to this place or time; it was somewhere he had to find for himself.

As the grey, stone wall to his right became higher, Andrew's attention was drawn to the slope where a woodsman, accompanied by two black Labradors, was cutting the dead branches from an old tree. He looked down at Madge and clicked his teeth. Her tail wagged as he handed her a small, beef-flavoured biscuit. It was a rocky walk along the terraced way and he was concerned for her feet, but the look in his dog's eyes suggested no discomfort and Andrew smiled. Her tail wagged more furiously.

He looked back at the faces he remembered from over the years, and recalled how they had impinged upon his life and his way of thinking. He thought of the many compromises he had had to make in order to accommodate their point of view or in order not to embarrass them, or in order to make things run smoothly, or in order to "do this one thing, just once, for me". He accepted, now, that these compromises had been his responsibility, and not that of those who had thrust them upon him. He couldn't talk his way back because they saw him as he had portrayed himself, and would only be able to respond to what had been – at least in part – a false image. In the end – in speech and manner – he had become a parody of what he, as a young man, had envisaged.

He reached out and stroked the green moss from the shoulder-high stone wall. The moss was soft and velvety. To his right, fresh stream water flowed into a small crevice by the side of the path. He scooped a mouthful and led Madge to drink. Around the little pool of water, ivy grew amongst the bracken but all else, including the trees on the slope, was bare and brown.

If he had created a prison of his marriage, it was a prison of his own making. No one had been his jailer; no one had denied him the key to his cell. It was not incumbent upon him to grit his teeth and see it through. He had travelled a long way with his family, he had done for them what he could; he had done his duty – as he saw it – to them, and now it was up to him to do his duty to himself. Others must judge him as they would – with scathing eloquence if it suited them, or with the degree of trust he felt he had earned.

We were not in the world to please other people at the expense of our own beliefs; if we lived to do so, we had only ourselves to blame for the outcome. Andrew harboured no bitterness, now. He felt himself slipping her coat around his wife's shoulder and opening the door for her to find the world she'd always wanted – for Mary, too, had her vision of what life should be and now she – as well as he – was free to make the search. Their children were old enough to care for themselves and find their own salvation.

The two of them – the man and his dog – passed through a final gate, and Andrew noticed how even the hard stone walls, rock solid for centuries, were buckling under the weight of the surrounding earth. In places, some of the stones, which had been so carefully and skilfully laid, had collapsed on to the footpath. From now on, though, the track was downhill. There was to be no more climbing. Ahead was Rydal Mount with its wonderful garden – a garden that seemed part of the natural landscape, a garden that seemed an effortless joy – and, beyond that, the Badger Bar.

On Christmas morning, Andrew woke at his usual time – early – and, as always, fed Madge before boiling himself two perfect eggs, which he ate with a rustic loaf.

He had chosen to cook a Lakeland dish – stuffed loin of pork – for his dinner and to accompany it with the usual trimmings. It took him less than half-an-hour to prepare the stuffing and place the dish, on the timer, in the oven. He parboiled the potatoes ready for roasting when he returned; he would then stir fry the sprouts with bacon and chestnuts. He smiled at Madge who always took an interest in any food preparation; she had watched him prepare the game soup on their return from Rydal the day before. He looked around the little kitchen of the cottage: the batter was waiting for the yorkshires, and the stollen slice, which he would serve with brandy butter, stood ready.

He pulled on his wax coat, stuffed a hip flask and some snacks for Madge in his pocket and set out for Easedale Tarn; it would take three hours to the tarn and back. It had been a favourite walk of Wordsworth's – one he undertook many times with his sister, Dorothy.

They passed a gateway across which, at shoulder height, was propped, horizontally, a barren stick. Into the stick, someone had burned, with great care, the message 'PLEASE LEAVE, IT KEEPS DEER OUT'. Andrew laughed: everyone, he thought, has their problems. A large slab of slate bridged the stream as they turned from the road to begin the ascent of the tarn. It was early, and he and Madge were alone. He looked back and watched her making her way across the wooden bridge and then, with great care, down the stone steps to the track where he stood waiting.

The Lakeland fells – grey stone and purple heather in the morning light – stretched before them. The track was rough and scattered with scree. He watched Madge pick her way between the stones, reluctant to put her on the lead in case it hampered her progress but aware of the sheep around them on the purple slopes. The path wound its way ever higher, following the course of the stream, and the walls that bordered it were bulged and twisted.

The waterfall at Sour Milk Gill appeared suddenly – although they had heard its winter roar from far back on the pony track – and Andrew stood watching the white waters crash into the river below. It was here that the poet, cheered by the sight of a rainbow, had been inspired to write the lines 'my heart leaps up when I behold a rainbow in the sky', and where he had hoped that it might always be so. The poem also contained those chilling lines 'the child is father of the man' and, once again, Andrew hoped that he had not let his children down during their growing years.

Sodden wet underfoot, they viewed the tarn, crossed the stepping stones and saw the boggy ground before them. Madge looked up, but with downcast eyes. Wet ground wasn't a favourite of hers, but Andrew didn't fancy the wide sweep left which would avoid it and so he lifted her in his arms and carried her to the bridge over Easedale Gill, from where they made their way back to the cottage. On the way, he noticed that the ridge of Fairfield, beyond Rydal Fell, was covered in snow.

Once inside, with the door shut firmly behind them, Andrew removed his boots, hung his wax coat on the door and rubbed Madge down until she was dry enough to steam lightly before the log fire, which he soon had blazing. He changed into dry clothes, drew shut the curtains, turned on the wall lights, poured a large whisky and cooked his Christmas dinner at a leisurely pace.

He ate the meal at the table by the sitting room fire – such was the habit of so many years – and washed it down with some mulled wine. All the while, Madge snored gently, content to be tired and asleep. The whole cottage was warm by now, and Andrew, also, began to doze. Outside, the dark had closed in and the winter's night was cold and bleak; inside, he felt invulnerable – protected from the world.

CHAPTER 25

The house

When Andrew arrived home at the cottage in Chelmondiston, a letter from Mary was waiting on the doormat. It was urgent, she said, and she must see him at once; she and the children would be waiting when 'he got back from his holiday'. Having known her as long as he had, Andrew did not miss the tone of the final phrase, and the assumptions from which it sprang.

The next day, when he arrived at the house that had been his family home, the door was opened by Mary, who led him immediately into their front room. There was no sign of Robert, but Jonathan and Amy were sitting on the settee, and they were not smiling. He failed to understand the apparent hostility that emanated from their eyes, and was reminded of the scene in the church when they had all turned and stared at him from the pew. He had loved these people, he had brought them up as well as he was able, he had spent time and energy and care upon them, and yet they sat as strangers might, staring him out.

"Would you like a cup of tea? We've had ours. You are rather later than we expected."

Again, he caught the tone and resented it. It stemmed from her humiliation, of course; he could see that, but not the need for this hostility. Couldn't just one of these sensitive, intelligent people understand him? Did he need someone to understand ... and pity him? Couldn't he go on alone just long enough for them to come round – if not to his way of thinking, then – at least – to an understanding of his motives? He had thought so in the Lakes. Perhaps distance eased the pain?

"I'm all right, thanks," he replied, trying to be reassuring, "You said it was urgent."

"I can't go on living here," snapped Mary, "the house is too big for me to manage on my own, and since you haven't replied to any of my letters and seem hell bent ... "

"Mum," said Jonathan, soothingly.

"Well, he makes me angry."

Andrew could see the anger in her eyes; behind the bewilderment and the humiliation lurked the rage. Layer upon layer of negative emotions were lined up against him, and his children had been conscripted to augment the attack. 'Where is it now, the glory and the dream?' He smiled to himself; there was always a sense of relief when he indulged in bitter humour. All the same, it hadn't started out like this; they had shared a dream, and the childhood years had been part of the glory they envisaged as a young couple. He was glad that Robert was safe in St Petersburg; he would not have liked this meeting.

Mary brought him a cup of tea with some biscuits, despite his refusal, and Andrew sat in what had been his favourite armchair – the one by the bay window – and watched Mary join her children on the settee.

"We need to discuss finances. If we have to give up the family home, then I need to be secure, and I need somewhere big enough to give the children a home while they need it. I shall need, at least, a four bed-roomed house."

"I haven't given this any thought ..." he began.

"Obviously – or we wouldn't be in this mess."

"I mean I haven't thought through the financial side of things. I assume we will split whatever we get from selling the house fifty-fifty."

"You won't need a large place, will you – if there's just you, and if there's someone else, then she can pay her share. She must be quite well off ..."

"Mum – let's keep this to the finances."

"Your father doesn't deny it."

"I'm going. Mary ..."

"Oh, that's right – just walk out. Is that how you deal with everything, Andrew – by walking away from it?"

"I agree to a fifty-fifty split of whatever we get from the house. We've already said that we'll find the tuition fees for the children – and that's a separate matter. We've said we'll find it, and we will. As things stand at the moment, they'll have to pay back any loan they take out for accommodation and food and so on – but we'll pay the tuition fees. We all sat down and discussed it ..."

"There's no need to shout."

He wasn't shouting – he was fairly sure of that; it was one of Mary's standard accusations when she wanted to ignore what he'd said, or unseat the points he made. He finished drinking his tea, and stood to leave.

"The house isn't all. There's your parents' money."

"My parents' money – they're still alive?"

"But you'll inherit when they die, and it isn't fair that it should go to another woman. I've looked after them when they've come to stay. I've put up with your father …"

"Is this seemly – discussing what someone might leave you when they're still alive?"

"I don't see why someone else should benefit. When my parents died, the money they left me went into this house. It may not have been much but …"

"Mary – this is all going over my head. I'll discuss it with my parents, but …"

"You'll do no such thing. I'm talking about the money they leave you. I think I'm entitled to half of it for putting up with them all these years."

"Yes – right. I'm happy for a fifty-fifty split of anything we own, but I'm not sure we should be discussing my parents' money …"

"It would help the children pay off their loans."

Andrew looked at Jonathan and Amy. Their expressions had not changed – except, perhaps, to have assumed the emotions conveyed by Mary's eyes – bewilderment, humiliation and anger. The word 'implacable' crossed his mind, and Andrew did not smile; there was no humour left, even of the dark kind. He wanted to go, now; he wanted to get out of his home and away, for a time, while he collected his thoughts. He could appreciate Mary's sense of panic – she always panicked if she feared the flow of money was going to dry up – but he couldn't believe that his children were complicit in what she suggested.

"It's not right that you – and she – should have all the money, and that I should have none. I've worked too hard to be poor in my old age. You shouldn't have done it, Andrew. There was no need for this …"

Andrew saw that Jonathan was standing, his arms around his mother; he saw Amy follow suit. And yet, what did he do? There had been a need. He had a right to be free from verbal abuse, from constant dissatisfaction, from never coming up to someone else's mark, from having what he could and couldn't say or do circumscribed ... but he had no right to abandon her. Andrew accepted the dilemma, but saw no remedy except the endless talking over of 'problems' – talking that led nowhere. He reached the door that led into the hall, and turned to look at his family.

"You don't need to worry about the money," he said, "it will be done fairly."

Somehow, he realised that they knew it was true. Looks could mean everything, or be simply expressions of the moment. Family ties went deeper than looks; they were implicit 'and far more deeply interfused'.

"Don't put the phone down," she pleaded, "please just listen for a few minutes. Give me a few minutes. I think I deserve that."

It was the following day – New Year's Day – and Andrew had known it was Mary before he lifted the receiver. He had spent the whole of New Year's Eve trying to square things in his head; his sense of freedom and of being at one with his world – so pervasive in the Lake District – had vanished overnight.

When he was young, he had imagined his ideal woman – the one he would love and cherish, with whom he would raise a family and who he would be happy to call his wife – but Mary had not matched up to that ideal. Marriage had not matched up to that ideal, and he had abandoned it; abandoned it after almost a quarter of a century of trying to make it work it was true, but abandoned it, nonetheless.

Abandoned, forsaken, discarded, deserted, rejected, cast off: that was how Mary felt. He had lost all wisdom in the matter and was following brute instinct, but even Andrew – at one of the lowest points in his life – could see the truth.

"I can't stand this vacuum between us," he heard her voice say on the other end of the phone, but he had heard it before, been there before, talked it endlessly through before, and all to no avail; life took over the next day, and they had carried on as before.

"If there is any hope that you may have made a mistake or changed your mind, please tell me."

Oh, he had changed his mind and made mistakes so many times; now, he was tired of it all.

"We could still sell the house and, in time, remember only the happier times of our life together."

So, she acknowledged that there had been happy times. Thank God: it was good to have that assurance from someone else.

"We could buy a smaller home away from it all …"

Away from what all? He hadn't wanted to get away from his home and his family – he loved his home and his family; he had wanted to get away from the constant sound of her voicing, carping and abusing. They used to call it 'nagging', but it was more than that; it was the desperate and insistent desire to impose one's will upon another human being. 'I'm cold' – meaning she wasn't capable, or didn't want, to make the decision to switch the heating on, 'the grass needs cutting' – meaning get out the lawnmower, at the end of another exhausting week, because we have guests coming, 'the house needs decorating' – meaning that would be easier for her than spring cleaning, 'you never listen to me' – after he'd sat three hours every week night listening to how difficult she found her job, 'most men ...' Andrew switched off his grievances: to go on piling them up was just a self-lacerating process.

"... put a bit in the bank and be comfortably off ..."

But we never would be because you would find ways of living up to our income. One holiday a year would become two, two would become three because your sister was having three ... and then we could 'just do this' or 'just do that', and then you'd wonder – in that feigned-innocent manner of yours – 'where the money had gone'.

"... you don't have to be retired to enjoy yourself – it's how you feel inside. I never felt old. I always tried to look after myself. I don't want to end up a 'poor old thing'. Elspeth and Brian are off to Paris at half-term; Sue from work is marrying her partner. She's nearly the same age as me. Why did I have to be abandoned at 46? ... Are you listening?"

"Yes."

"I wouldn't have pulled you down. There could be a new beginning and a rescuing of the pain of the last year. We could go forward with optimism ... I never stopped you doing what you wanted to do. Believe me, I would have loved you to have found a pleasurable interest years ago; perhaps this awful thing wouldn't have happened had you had another outlet. And certainly I would have enjoyed you taking me out to your social gatherings, when all I had to do was dress up instead of always being the one to create friends and company ... Are you listening?"

"Yes."

"I find it so upsetting when you say 'it isn't like that' or 'we never hold hands anymore' ... What's going on, Andy?"

"Nothing is going on."

"What's gone awry? You know where I'm coming from but where the hell are you, Andy? ... Are you listening?"

"Yes."

"Please don't sacrifice our happiness on a wobbly stone, Andy. She's using you. She can't give you any more than I have. All I want is you back but, if you can't – as it seems you can't – then help me to understand why you won't come and what I have done. It's not fair – you don't know what she'll be like in twenty years' time. She's bound to be wonderful now – the waves of life haven't tossed against the stony shore ... Please help me to understand ..."

He didn't put the phone down. He listened all morning, and then excused himself because Madge needed to go for a walk.

Andrew let himself into the house in Tuddenham Road for the last time. It was empty now, and he was due to hand the keys over to the estate agent on the following morning. He tipped the bunch of keys into his pocket and shut the door, quietly; even so, the slight sound echoed in the hollow house and Andrew felt (without acknowledging it to himself in words) that he was entering somewhere from which the spirit had departed.

Their house, near as it was to the Christchurch Park, had sold rapidly but without giving either of them enough, once the mortgage had been paid off, to buy somewhere of a similar size without mortgaging themselves into their seventies. Mary, after much wrangling, settled upon a three bed-roomed bungalow near Rushmere Heath golf course, and Andrew decided to stay where he was, renting the cottage for the time being.

The process of selling their family home had taken its toll. He had been tempted to take on the house, but the mortgage would have been huge, eating into a decent but not overly-generous salary. Both had been aware that their children would still need financial support – whatever they might say to the contrary. Tuition fees were rising, the cost of student accommodation was rising and the cost of living was rising. It was a bad time to be helping your children through university and conducting a divorce. More decisive than his worry over the effects of the cost, however, was Andrew's fear that something quite irreplaceable would leave with the family.

His love for the house bordered upon rapture. An early girlfriend of Jonathan's had once commented that houses were 'just bricks and mortar'. Andrew believed – and knew, from their unspoken looks, his family shared the belief that the young woman had missed the point entirely. Once lived in and once loved, houses took on a special spirit of their own, which reflected the souls of those for whom they had been home.

This was the home in which the things of real importance in his life had occurred. He and Mary had settled in quickly as a young married couple, and here each of their children had been conceived in love. It was here that he had taken his first steps as painter, carpenter and general handyman. It was here that Mary had first turned her hands to making curtains and knitting throws. It was here that they had created the nursery to which they had brought each of their children. Andrew remembered carrying Jonathan to the little cot Mary's father had made, and wondering how he was ever going to rear this little bundle of life. He recalled Robert stumbling down the stairs, one hand over his left eye, and wondering why so much blood was pouring through his child's fingers: it was only a cut on the boy's forehead brought about by boisterous play in the bedroom, but the sight had terrified Andrew.

He took his eyes from the stairs, and walked through the house and out into the back garden where the first pets had been housed – Amy's guinea pigs, Robert's tortoise and Jonathan's rabbits. He walked over the patio he had dug out and cast his eyes over the garden he – and, at first, Mary – had landscaped and tended. It was an attractive garden, long and narrow, and wound its way through arbours and arches to the vegetable plot where the children had planted their first seeds. Here they had brought their friends – one of whom had commented on what a welcoming home it was – and here they had created games of skill and imagination with the dressing-up box and the plastic figures and the sheer energy of children. On the old aviary, he saw the soldier's hat Robert had found in that French river; Andrew eased the nail that held it from the wood and took the metal hat with him.

Leaving the back door unlocked, Andrew wandered into the house, knowing he should not have come but realising that he was right to have done so. He laughed at his own contradiction; there was something of that, he thought, in his nature.

The open fireplace in the lounge beckoned him with remembered Christmases and birthdays; he recalled wrapping paper strewn everywhere and the excited cries of his children. Even as very young ones they had taken a delight in each other's pleasures, with no sign of envy. He had been proud of them, then as now.

On the first landing, their bedrooms – in which Andrew had read them all to sleep – opened his heart: Jonathan's, where everything was placed in almost an old-maidish tidiness but which was full of board games that enlivened the winter evenings: Roberts, where he had kept his finches in a fitted wardrobe for fear that the outside aviary was too cold in winter: Amy's, strewn – during her young teens – with clothes and make-up and CDs.

The house held these memories – marked by holes in the plaster and stains on the floor and hooks from the ceiling – and the house led him on, through the kitchen where Mary had taught them all to cook, through the bathroom where he had first washed each of them with a tenderness in his heart that overwhelmed him, and downstairs to the back parlour – the untidy room, where they had romped, where Madge had joined in the fun and where the old cat, which Amy had found under the garden hedge one winter's night, found its final, cosy resting place behind the faded armchair.

He came at last to what had become his study but which had started out as a games room. The snooker table had been here, and the darts board and – in the cupboards – the old-fashioned games such as bar skittles, shove-halfpenny and bagatelle. Here, as young teens with their friends, they had drunk their first alcohol, lounging on the sloppy sofa that doubled as a bed or, on warm nights, spilling out into the garden. Here, too, Andrew kept his books – shelf upon shelf of them

– which gradually found their way to his children's bedrooms as they became old enough to read them.

It was here that Andrew had done most of his quiet thinking – once the house was closed down and everyone was safe in bed. Sitting at the old wooden desk, (rescued by his father from an insurance company's discarded furniture) Andrew had plotted his school plays, organised his working life, thought through his family's problems, pored over holiday brochures, studied maps and written the diaries that had kept him sane over the years; during this time he had progressed from an old manual typewriter to his current word-processor.

There was a comfortable warmth about this room that conjured all his feelings as soon as he entered. It was due, partly, to the wooden furniture, but more to the fact that this particular room had never experienced an argument. Mary had taken him aside, to give him whatever bollocking she felt necessary at the time, into every other room of the house that was out of anyone's immediate hearing – but he had never allowed such a thing to happen here. Only once, when his sister-in-law and brother-in-law had arrived unexpectedly to find them in the throes of dissent and found Andrew in tears at his desk, had this room experienced anything like discord. Tears, yes – he had cried quietly to himself many times – but never harshness and disaffection.

Once, during that night, he ventured out to walk the roads that led from, to and around Christchurch Park with its open spaces where his children had played, and through which they wandered into the town. He looked up at the stars and, realising his smallness, was lost in the infinity of existence.

He stalked the rooms with their memories, ran his hands lovingly over the walls and kissed them. He huddled in corners like a trapped animal ready to defend itself. He placed his hands on window sills scarred with Madge's claws, and looked out into the night. He sat peacefully, recalling the happy times in each of the rooms. He spread-eagled himself on the floors and asked that someone, somewhere, might know the truth and pity him.

During the night, he wrote a note to the new owners, telling them that they had bought a home once filled with love and in which, he hoped, they too would find happiness and come to know the house as he and his family had done.

Mostly, however, he spent his time in that room – his special room – and sobbed until he could sob no more. His heart was as full as the house was now empty. His heart felt as a heart in love feels – as though it could burst with the emotion. Andrew's ardour racked him until he could choke and cry no longer. The tears dried on his face, and he rubbed them aside carelessly.

When morning came, and before anyone was about, he checked all the rooms and locked the house securely. Standing on the pavement, looking back at what had once been his home, Andrew wished – he hoped, not foolishly – that, one day, it might be so again: if not, then perhaps someone would be kind enough to scatter his ashes in the garden.

CPSIA information can be obtained at www.ICGtesting.com
Printed in the USA
LVOW10s1135261015

459775LV00001B/25/P

9 781781 489741